Visions of Whereafter

By

David Muir

James McKeever faces a stark choice: "... perhaps *this* is reality and it was my life that has been a dream?"

Cover design by Philippa Lobban

Visions of Whereafter
By
David Muir

© David Muir, September 2012

Acknowledgements

My heartfelt thanks go to my wife, Annette, for her support while I was engaged in researching and writing this book and for her editing skills. Thanks also go to Peter Lobban for designing and managing my author's website and a special thanks goes to Philippa Lobban for her wonderful cover design.

David Muir, Solihull, December 2012.

Chapter One

The Guardians

'Where am I?' I hear myself say out loud, finding myself sitting in a white, leather armchair in a small, white room with no visible means of entry or exit.

'You are in a small, white room with no visible means of entry or exit', comes the reply from behind a chest-high, white counter positioned at the opposite side of the room from where I am sitting. At first I hadn't seen the only other occupant of the room, or his counter, in my bleary-eyed state.

'I do apologise sir,' he continues, 'sometimes, I can't help myself. Everyone asks that question at first ... it gets *very* predictable. But since you ask, you are in Lounge 9000 and I am your Guardian.'

This matter-of-fact explanation is offered by a tall, white-haired man, dressed in a bespoke grey suit, holding what looks like a white clipboard and pen in his left hand.

'9000 ... *Guardian*?', I ask.

'Correct sir. May I see your papers?'

'Papers?'

'The envelope that you are clutching to your chest; may I see it sir?' I hand over the envelope without protest, noticing the numerals nine zero zero zero printed in a large font on its outside.

'Everyone is a bit confused to begin with sir.'

'Confused … just a bit!', I reply.

'This way for your transport sir.'

'Transport?'

'Are you going to repeat *everything* I say sir?'

'No … look … no, I'm sorry … I'll try not to, but I *really* am very confused.'

'I know. That is what I am saying. Everyone is … '

'Yes, you said.' I cut him off in mid-sentence. 'This is all very puzzling you know.'

My apparent Guardian beckons me to stand up and follow him towards the counter he emerged from a few moments ago. He picks up a briefcase from the counter top and taps an unseen panel on the wall near the counter and an equally unseen door silently opens on to what is best described as an underground railway station. A single, long train carriage, decked out in red and grey livery, is stationed at the only platform. Other baffled-looking individuals are being escorted quietly by their grey-suited Guardians from adjacent lounges towards a series of open carriage doors.

Then I see it: the logo splashed across the side of the carriage. '*Virgin*!', I exclaim loudly.

'Yes sir,' confirms my Guardian, 'the idea came from a former employee of Sir Richard who has been here for quite some time. The trouble is … ' he leans towards me and drops his voice to a whisper, 'the trouble is, these trains are often late. Nothing we can do. We're stuck with it. He's got the monopoly. We are in luck … this one's on time. Let's get aboard.'

'Where are we going?', I ask.

'All in good time sir; you'll be taken care of.' My Guardian gestures me to sit down opposite him on one of the plush banquettes that line the carriage, hands back the envelope and detaches the white pen from its holder and uses it to operate his electronic clipboard. The device beeps and burbles in response to touches of his pen. 'Hold on to it please sir, they will need your envelope later.'

'*They* will?'

'You're doing it again sir.'

'Sorry,' I reply, 'I can't help it.'

The carriage doors close silently and we move swiftly and noiselessly along a brightly-lit tunnel. My Guardian reaches into his briefcase that is lying on the banquette next to him and hands me a glossy leaflet. *Elvis Impersonation Contest*, it reads: *Tonight in the Town Hall, Morlham.* 'I thought that you might be interested in this sir? You will be able to catch it if you wish after you settle in; it's one of our regular events.'

'Don't they get a bit predictable?' I venture, resisting the urge to repeat "settle in".

'Oh no, many of our guests enjoy them. Elvis sometimes turns up and enters.'

'*What*!' I exclaim, 'that's unfair. He would win every time.'

'Not necessarily sir. The last time he entered, he came in third.'

Whilst I am digesting this baffling revelation, my Guardian continues: 'In any case, Elvis always comes in disguise.'

'How the hell does he disguise himself for an Elvis impersonation contest?'

'Easily sir, he dresses up much like the others. Consequently, no-one recognises him.'

Although I'm still struggling to take this in, a thought occurs to me. 'What about Jim? Can you put me in contact with Jim? I used to work with him.'

'I'll need some details sir, full name and so forth,' answers my Guardian. He pulls what I take to be a tablet computer from his briefcase, places it on his lap and proceeds to tap and stroke the screen of the thin, white device.

'This kind of device can be voice activated,' my Guardian informs me, 'but I don't wish to disturb our fellow passengers more than is necessary.'

After a few moments of tapping and stroking, my Guardian looks up from his tablet computer and is ready with an answer: 'Ah yes, found him. In fact I can tell you exactly what Jim spends most of his time doing. He rides a massive motorbike on the desert highways, his long hair flowing behind him.'

'Hair flowing,' I mutter, 'that means he's not wearing a helmet. That could get him killed.'

'You forget sir', says my Guardian, leaning towards me and placing a reassuring hand on my left knee, 'that's partly how your Jim got here in the first place. It can't happen again. Please excuse me for a moment, I have to send a text message to someone.

'In point of fact,' my Guardian lowers his voice so that occupants of adjacent banquettes don't hear him, 'Jim knows where Elvis has a regular gig. It's at a bar somewhere out in the desert. Not many people know where it is. I'm reliably informed that Johnny Cash sometimes gigs with the King. That must be quite a night.' My Guardian leans back and a faint smile crosses his countenance in response to my beaming face.

I notice that the carriage is silent; I had almost forgotten about my fellow passengers, in whom I seem strangely uninterested. Whilst I am reflecting on my apparent lack of concern for the other 'arrivals', the train emerges from the tunnel into bright daylight. The train is travelling swiftly and smoothly along the side of a gently sloping valley that is lined with dense woods above the railway track and green fields and stone walls below it. A sparkling river meanders along the bottom of the valley below us. The opposite slope of the valley is similarly embossed with an irregular lattice of stone walls and I can just make out a road on the opposite side of the valley just above the river. From time to time the train traverses stone bridges that span narrower, side valleys that merge with the main valley revealing hamlets and villages in the clefts created by the joining of valleys and moors. There are the occasional farm and cottage to be seen between the villages that dot the floor of the main valley.

'This could be one of the Yorkshire Dales,' I suggest to my Guardian.

'Lovely isn't it. This whole region, apart - obviously - from the desert that I mentioned before, is actually modelled on the Yorkshire Dales. We are nearly there. The nearest town to where you are going is coming up, if you look down now.'

The train slows down a little and passes over a high stone viaduct that spans a wide valley that is large enough to host a small town.

'The town of Morlham is down there,' points out my Guardian. 'We are about to pass through its station, but we are not stopping on this occasion.'

The viaduct takes the train high over the town above a long, narrow marketplace.

'There are lots of local food stalls; wine and cheese and the like,' says my Guardian. 'It is easy to get to from where you will be living; it's not far. We will be there very soon.'

'The town looks very much like somewhere I have been to in northern France,' I say to my Guardian, 'Morlaix.'

'Well spotted sir, we tend to model places on known places, if you take my meaning.'

After passing over Morlham, the main valley widens and we pass a number of villages to our right on the valley floor. At length, the train slows down and come to a halt.

'This is our station, your destination', announces my Guardian.

I follow my Guardian obediently to the nearest open carriage door and step out behind him on to a short, wooden platform. The train's single carriage moves swiftly and noiselessly away before I realise that we are the only occupants who have left the train.

The station platform is positioned near the foot of the slope of one side of the wooded valley into which the train emerged from the tunnel earlier in my journey. The other side of the valley is some distance ahead of me and between its two sides a large village nestles on the valley floor.

'What about the others and what is this place?' I enquire of my Guardian who has been standing patiently next to me while I have been taking in my immediate surroundings.

'They have other destinations in mind,' comes the vague reply. 'This is where you will stay for a while until you make up your mind,' he announces. I ignore the bit about *making up my mind* and marvel at the reality of his pronouncement. The light is very bright and there is a warm breeze. What I have called the village spreads out below us across a large, semi-elliptical, grassy area that is criss-crossed by neat, gravelled walkways. These join a number of cottages and houses, some of which are of remarkable design. Before I have a chance to quiz my Guardian about them, he gestures towards a wide walkway that leads from the station platform down to the village. 'There is someone to see you down there.'

Before I have time to take in any more of my surroundings, I see Jim a few yards ahead of me at the foot of the slope sitting astride an enormous motorbike. To my relief he *is* wearing a helmet, but his hair is as long as I remember it and falls down his back below the level of his head protection: long enough to flow behind him when his bike is in motion, I imagine. I want to run the last few yards across the intervening space and hug him, but someone else is. There is no mistaking the platinum blond hair and the hourglass figure inside skin-tight, black biker's leathers. She releases herself from Jim, says something to him and gives me a cheery wave before sashaying away. I fight the urge to follow her with my eyes, but I give up and stare at her in amazement.

'It's … it's … great to see you Jim. If that is who I think it is … was … what … what the hell are you doing with her on the back of your motorbike?' My words come tumbling out.

'She likes going for long, fast rides on the desert highways. Good to see you too man; how the hell are you?'

'Er … confused; I can't figure out what is going on here.'

'No worries, your man will explain stuff as and when you need,' says Jim from an evident position of knowledge and experience. 'When you are settled in … you've got one of the houses on the other side of the village green … I'll call for you. Have I got a surprise for you this evening.'

'I don't think that I can take any more surprises Jim. It's been a very odd day, if this actually *is* a *day*.'

'See you later man.' Jim rides off in the direction of what looks like a large, open gate a hundred or so yards away to my left.

'Looking well, isn't he sir,' says my Guardian, who has been waiting patiently watching the brief reunion. 'I need to give you this.' He pulls a slim, smartphone from his inside suit pocket and hands it to me. 'There isn't a manual; it is highly intuitive. The screen icons more or less tell you what's what. Look, there is even an icon of me; there's my face with my name – Kal – below it.'

'Hey, this looks pretty much like an iPhone™,' I exclaim before slipping it into my inside pocket, noticing the suit's label. 'How did I acquire this expensive suit and why is the 'phone so thin?'

'Correct sir. We blatantly stole the design from Steve Jobs long before he arrived here. We simply couldn't resist using the design. He could hardly have sued us, could he?' Kal allows himself a satisfied chuckle. 'As to the suit ... we know what you like. There are lots more in your house. You'll find a pair of Ray Bans™ in the top pocket if you find the sunlight here too bright.'

'But it's black,' I state obviously, 'the 'phone I mean; this goes against the colour scheme of personal belongings around here.'

'We're waiting for the white ones to come in sir. Mister Jobs, now that he is here, is heavily involved in the design of these communicating devices: everyone has them. This one, the current version, is known as the iPhone 12. The reason why it is very slim is because it is made from graphene.'

'If you tap my icon you will be able to communicate with me by means of text, voice or video. I'll show you how later. You can call me anytime, day or night. This is particularly important when you have made up your mind or if you want to change your mind.

'It can be activated by voice, or by tapping and stroking the screen in the way in which you are probably familiar with smartphones in general. I'll explain how the voice activation works later, when we are in your house.'

'Graphene ... that's at least twice that you have referred to me changing my mind. I don't quite understand: about what?'

'All will become clear in time sir. Let's wait and see. You will get the hang of it. Let us go and announce your arrival.'

My Guardian leads the way along one of the paths, across what Jim referred to as the village green, towards a low building where we will, apparently, announce my arrival. On the way, I take the opportunity to glance at some of the other buildings that line the smooth curve of the green. 'That must be a Le Corbusier and those two are Frank Lloyd Wright houses.'

'You know your architects sir. What do you think of the Mackintosh house?'

'It's a very fine example. I assume that you take advantage of their presence here.'

'You will be staying in the Mackintosh sir, until ...'

'... I change my mind?' I venture.

The revolving doors of the single-storey building that we have been walking towards give onto what looks like a hotel lobby. Another grey-suited man, standing behind a reception desk, asks me for my envelope; I hand it over, realising that I am still clutching it. He takes it and hands me a white folder. 'Everything about your house and your surroundings is explained in here sir,' he says gracefully.

Kal indicates that we can leave and we emerge back onto the green. I can see the Mackintosh house more clearly from this angle. 'I will show you briefly round your house and explain a few things so that you can settle in to your new surroundings.

'The front and back doors of your house can be opened by placing your palm over the door pad. It won't work for anyone else, just your palm print. You try it.'

I notice that the door jamb for my front door is fitted with what looks like a pad of some kind at shoulder height. I place my palm over it; the mechanism makes a satisfying electronic click.

'You will find that the door handle will work now that it has scanned your palm. When you close the door behind you when you leave the house, it locks automatically. The same goes for any of the doors. We don't get any burglaries, but locking the door seems to keep residents happy. Let's go in.'

'No burglaries?'

'None at all sir. After you sir.'

I decide to add the mystery of how my door knows *my* palm print by adding this fact to the legion of other mysteries and questions that jumble about in my mind and attempt to concentrate on one thing at a time: I open the door and step into a light and airy, wide hallway. There are items of furniture in the unmistakable style of Charles Rennie Mackintosh set against the walls: a chair here, an elegant table there. Door handles and light fittings also bear the hallmark of Mackintosh design.

'The house looks lovely Kal.'

'Indeed it is sir,' comes his voice behind me. 'It is a very fine house. I think that you will enjoy your stay here.

'If we go through the first door on the left, we can sit down and have a chat. I want to explain a few things to you. Let's sit over there.'

I sit meekly opposite Kal in one of two armchairs that are placed near a wide bay window that overlooks the village green.

'Now James, I know that you must be bursting with questions. You have just arrived here and you will be confused, concerned and quite possibly much more besides. May I suggest that you let me do the talking for now ... that might answer some of your questions.' Kal settles back in his armchair and begins.

'Let's deal with some practicalities. I know that you want to know how you got here and why it is that you have met someone who is, for all intents and purposes, *dead*. I want to put Jim and, for that matter, Elvis Presley to one side for the moment and deal with some day-to-day matters so that you can begin to settle in here. We can deal with these other things - hugely important though they are - at a later date. Is that all right with you?'

I nod and let Kal continue.

'To make life understandable here, there is a twenty four hour day. There are seven days in a week and so forth. Anything associated with time is, therefore, familiar to you ... the same as before. There is a calendar on the wall in your kitchen. I've marked today's date, the day of your arrival.'

'What year is it Kal?'

'Ah, I thought that you might ask me that.

'The year is divided into twelve months as before. However, the number of the year won't mean anything to you. It is, in fact, five thousand and fifty.'

Kal holds up a hand to stifle my obvious question. 'Let me proceed.

'So, that has dealt with time to some extent. As I've said, the main reason for this arrangement is so that new arrivals can settle in quickly. Have you looked at your watch yet?'

I notice, for the first time, that I am wearing a fine-looking watch. 'No, not yet. It's almost mid-day. Nice watch.'

'It has an everlasting battery.

'Next: paying for things. There is a list in your folder of numbers that you can call from your communicator for the usual goods and services. If anything in your house goes wrong. there will be a number that you can call - day or night.

'If you press the icon with the outline of a human head on, this will take you to your contacts page. I'm your only contact so far: there's my face. For each contact, you can choose voice, text or video communication. Do you see me as an entry in your contacts list?'

I nod. 'Yes, I've got you. How do I get back to ... oh, I've found it, I'm back to the main screen of icons. Your face is on the home screen as well.'

'Indeed so sir. As time goes by, you can save names and numbers of contacts. I'll leave you to find out how to save contacts. My icon is also on the main screen for ease of access to me. Its a special icon in that respect; that's why it is on the home screen.

'You will find that just about everything that you do with your communicator by tapping icons and stroking screens can also be done by voice activation. All that you have to do is to speak to it while you are holding it a short distance away from you, like this. You could try this when I've gone. Switching it on and off is also by voice activation. The battery won't run out; it will last for the lifetime of the device. If you experience any problems with your communicator, just pop into the office where we were a few minutes ago.

'There is a shop on the village green. May I suggest that you introduce yourself later on. The shop is very well-stocked and will get you anything that you need that isn't on the shelves. I have taken the liberty of arranging your fridge and larder to be stocked with provisions. I hope that they are to your liking.

'Let's get back to paying for things. This works only by voice activation. If you simply say "pay", a screen appears that includes a scrambled version of your personal details and your personal identification code.'

'What if I lose my smartphone,' I manage to interrupt Kal. 'Anyone could do this and use my personal code.'

'Your communicator will respond only to your voice once you have trained it to recognise your voice. A communicator cannot be re-trained, so it cannot respond to anyone else's voice. Let's try it. Say the word "pay" and see what happens. You may have to say it more than once because it is a new communicator and a new user. It will soon get used to your voice.'

I say the word "pay" three times before the screen refreshes. 'It now says "activated" at the top of the screen, but the details still look scrambled.'

'That's correct.' says Kal. If you say "back" or press the back button, I won't be able to use your communicator. It won't respond to my voice because it is now trained only to your voice and cannot be re-trained so it won't respond to anyone else's voice. Let me demonstrate.'

I hand my smartphone to Kal. He says "pay" several times and hands the device back to me.

'Right, I see. We are still on the home screen. If I now say "pay", the screen should change. Yes, it does. What is the purpose of this activated screen. It's still scrambled isn't it?'

'Yes it is. When you purchase anything from a shop either here or in Morlham, or when you are paying for some service or goods that are delivered to your door, the shopkeeper or whoever you are paying is equipped with a hand-held scanner. The merchant will scan your identification details and the amount will be debited from your account ... and before you ask, there are plenty of credits - as we call them here - in your account.'

'What happens when my credits run out, when I have no money left?'

'Don't worry about that sir. I will ensure that your account doesn't run out. And if you lose your communicator, let the office know and they will issue a new one. Remember that no-one else can voice activate your communicator, so no-one else will be able to access your credits if someone finding your communicator attempts to use it. In any event, we don't get this kind of problem: lost communicators are usually handed-in if found. We don't get that kind of crime here. Nevertheless, residents find it comforting if their communicators work only for them and no-one else to pay for things. It is easier to organise things that way, in a way that residents are happy with.'

'Really; no crime. That *is* interesting. And you mean to say that I can live here for free; I don't have to work or earn a living to pay for all of this?'

'For the time being sir, yes. You don't have to earn a living in the sense that you were used to it before. You can treat your time to come as a settling in period, a kind of assessment period.'

'Am I being assessed Kal? And for what?'

'Let's leave this kind of question to one side for now sir, shall we? Have a look around your house and village, familiarise yourself with your new surroundings. I would like you to enjoy your time here: celebrate you new life. I will come and see you tomorrow morning: I will 'phone first.

'By the way, there are other icons on your main and sub-screens for the weather, maps and so forth. I am sure that you will get the hang of using your communicator very quickly. Just think of it as a very smart, smartphone similar to those that you used previously. Remember that you can call me at any time, day or night.

'As for other mundane things such as water, gas and electricity, these are similar to what you were used to. LIving here, in practical terms, is similar to before. We don't have an energy crisis here. There is plenty for everyone and for everything. However, that is another story for another time perhaps.'

Kal has evidently finished his introductory chat with me and gets up from his chair and extends his right hand as I rise from my chair to face him.

'I think that you will find that your life here peaceful and harmonious.'

'Thank you Kal. Thank you for helping me ... it has been a fascinating day so far, baffling and wonderful in equal measure. I don't know what to make of it, but I have a lot to think about and to find out, not the least of which is the matter of getting something to eat. I think that I can manage that for myself though.'

'I will leave you for now sir. It will be better if I leave you to get acquainted with your house and your surroundings for the remainder of the day. Please have a look around the village, but please don't wander too far from it yet. Remember that your friend Jim is coming to see you this evening, so perhaps you should give the Elvis impersonation contest a miss: there will be others. You will find trainers and walking boots in one of the clothes cupboards upstairs if you want to go for a walk outside the village - not too far mind.

'Goodbye for now sir.' My Guardian leaves the room before I could ask any more questions or before I could tell him that Virgin

Trains has lost its franchise. I hear the front door close and I watch from my front room window as my Guardian strides quickly across the village green towards the reception building and disappears inside.

Chapter Two

Jim and the King

I spent several minutes looking out of the window after Kal left me to contemplate my new surroundings and my mysterious circumstances. The village green was devoid of other "residents", as Kal had referred to my, as yet unseen, neighbours. There was no doubting it, I felt alone in a strange place. Suddenly I remembered that I would see a friendly face this evening: Jim will be able to enlighten me as to why we are both here. With this thought in mind, I shook off my present anxiety and decided to look around my house.

My delight in the house could not have been greater: it is replete with Charles Rennie Mackintosh furniture and fittings, with the addition of a ultra-modern kitchen and bathroom that are also blessed with touches of the husband and wife team of Charles and Margaret Mackintosh's genius for design down to the smallest detail.

The house comprises two large rooms at the front, on either side of the central hall. One room is where I was listening to Kal and the other an elegant dining room. The kitchen is behind the room where we talked and to the rear of the dining room is a study-cum-library with French windows that open onto the back garden. I only glance quickly at the garden and plan to give it a closer examination later.

There are two bedrooms and a large bathroom on the first floor.

My first thought upon entering the kitchen was that I should find something to eat: I was suddenly aware that I was very hungry. It did not take me long to find some bread and cheese to make myself a simple meal at the kitchen table before venturing outside.

I retraced my steps towards the railway station where I encountered Jim earlier, climbed a few of the wooden steps and looked back towards the village. (Presumably I can catch a train to Morlham from here: something to ask Kal.)

My first impression of the village was that houses and cottages line the curved edge of the village green, behind which there is a stand of tall trees that affords glimpses of high moors beyond. The end building, nearest the railway station, is the office where Kal took me earlier and the village shop is next to it. The building at the other end of the row has the appearance of a village hall. It was the shop that I aimed for next and passed someone coming out just as I reached the door. This was my first encounter with another human being, apart from Kal and Jim and Jim's passenger. We exchanged pleasantries as I approached the avuncular shopkeeper standing behind his counter.

'My Guardian suggested that I let you know I am here. He said something about an account?'

'Yes, good afternoon sir. Are you staying in the Mackintosh house just along the green?'

'Yes, that's me. I'm James MacKeever.'

'Your account has been set up Mr. MacKeever. It simply means that you place any purchase on account and settle up at the end of the month. Has it been explained to you how you pay for things?'

'Yes. So, it's as simple as that. Your shop looks very well-stocked.'

'Thank you sir. If there is anything that you need that we don't have, please let me know. I can usually get it by the end of the day or in a day or two, depending on what it is. Is there anything that I can get for you today?'

'I don't think so. My Guardian has made sure that I am well stocked for food and toiletries to begin with; I seem to have everything I need for the time being.'

My local shopkeeper smiled broadly. 'Well, if there is anything I can get you, you know where we are Mr. MacKeever. Good-day to you.'

I turned and left the shop and returned to my house, passing three other properties along the way. The warm sun bathed the village in a soft light and I heard unseen birds singing as I approached my front door and let myself in. I leant against the door and closed my eyes for a few moments, hardly able to take everything in. There is so much that I want to know: perhaps Jim can help when I see him later.

❋

I was woken up from where I had dozed in an armchair by the chimes of the front door. Jim appeared on the front step. 'Are you ready to go, we should go soon,' he says with a slight note of impatience in his voice. 'Where did they put your leathers?'

Jim bounded upstairs as if he knew the layout of the house, leaving me standing in the hall. 'I didn't know that we were going out,' I called up to him.

In what seemed like no time at all, Jim reappeared with some dark blue biker's gear. 'Put these on. I hope that the boots fit. You won't need your smartphone; I've got mine ... I'll get the beers.'

'Let's go into the kitchen. Take a seat Jim. Do I put these on over my trousers?'

'Yeah, and the leather jacket over your shirt.'

'Do we have to go right now?' I asked Jim as I struggle into my leather trousers, 'there are some things that I must ask you. Hey, this leather is so soft. For instance, where the hell are we and where are we going this evening?'

'They look great,' said Jim. 'The jacket is a good fit and the colour is perfect. I have a spare helmet. As to where we are going, suffice it to say that it involves beer - low alcohol in my case - and music. You'll see when we get there.'

I sat down at the other kitchen chair opposite Jim.

'As to where are we, where do you think?'

'Kal doesn't say much on the subject neither do you. This place could be Utopia, but - by definition - such a place doesn't exist, it was the vision of Sir Thomas More in fifteen something or other.'

'Kal asked me not to say too much on the subject, I'm afraid James. I expect that he wants you to find out stuff for yourself. I could give you my view, after all I have been here for a few years and you probably think that I have come to some conclusions. However to be honest, I don't think about it that much; I prefer to celebrate life ... I assumed that I had lost it.'

'So you can't tell me where we are then.'

'Er, I prefer to go by Kal's wishes; he was very specific ... asked me not to say. Why don't you take things in for a while and then speak to Kal. There's no guarantee that he will enlighten you fully. You will just have to wait and see what he says.'

'That is not the first time that someone has said "wait and see" to me. Okay, I promise that I will wait and see for a few days, if indeed there are more days to wait for. In the meantime I'm looking forward to going out, so I'll try and forget about the "where are we?" problem and seize the moment. Who knows, there might not be too many more, I might wake up and find out that all this has been a dream.'

Jim laughed. 'Jacket on, boots on. You look great, let's go. My bike runs on advanced biofuel, by the way. Hardly any pollution.'

I climbed on to the pillion seat of Jim's motorbike and we set off slowly, across the walkway that leads from my house towards the road that runs alongside the far side of the green where I had met Jim earlier. Jim quickened the bike as we took the empty road past the edge of the village green towards the open gate that I had noticed this morning. As we approached this apparent boundary of the village, I noticed that the road that passes through the gate gave onto a region of low hills. Jim waved at the gateman who was sitting in a small hut.

'Harry is one of the gatemen for your village; he knows where we are going. This is the end of the main valley that you came along in the train,' explains Jim, 'after a few miles along here we reach the desert.'

The hills and valleys soon fell away to an almost flat, desert region where the road painted a black strip straight ahead across a sea of sand. As soon as we emerged from the hills onto the desert road, Jim kicked the bike into a higher gear so that we seem to leap onto the black highway, the sand a blur to either side of us.

'Hold tight,' yelled Jim, fighting against the roar of the bike, 'it's about forty miles.'

I held on and revelled in the speed and noise of the bike. 'Teach me how to ride one of these Jim,' I yelled back at him.

We soon left the main road that cuts across the desert and Jim expertly threw the bike into a number of lefts and rights until we left the tarmac behind and were bumping slowly along a dusty track to reach what is best described as a shabby-looking diner or bar of some kind. The diner, a low wooden building with a rickety wooden roof, is set back from the track, leaving space for a rough car park in front. Several ancient cars and a number of gleaming motorbikes were parked randomly amongst expensive-looking SUVs so that we had to weave our way through them to reach the steps of the diner. Once inside, I immediately warmed to the hubbub and shock of hearing several voices at once, the first time this has happened since my arrival.

'We can hang our gear over there.' Jim pointed to a row of hooks. Bike leathers and helmets dangled from them like men with bowed heads, waiting in a line for something to happen. We found a couple of vacant hooks next to one another and disrobed. 'We'll need something for our feet.' Jim pointed towards a row of leather slippers on a shelf above the hooks. 'Put these on, its much better than walking around in our socks. Don't worry, all the bikers wear them. I know it doesn't look cool, but it's better than sitting around in your boots. There's a table over there; I'll get some beers.' I noticed that Jim stopped to chat with several people and waved to others as he made his way towards the bar: he seemed to be well-known to most of the people here.

I sat down and tried to take in my surroundings. The bar was fairly full; I wondered if this was normal, as we seemed to be in a remote place in the desert. I immediately recognised some faces and vaguely recognised others. Then, with barely suppressed excitement, I saw Richard Feynman sitting at a table, surrounded by several young women, and there were Amy Winehouse and Kurt Cobain chatting excitedly at another.

'Who's Richard Feynman?', asked Jim, returning with four beers.

'Why have you got *four* beers? He is, or is that was, a *very* famous physicist,' I replied.

'Never heard of him,' said Jim. 'He's in here a lot though, likes the music. Talking of which, that's the reason I brought you here tonight. You are going to love the band. We were just in time. I'm glad you arrived when you did; we only just made it. Saves me queueing for the bar again.'

Almost on cue, the members of the band wandered on to the small stage at the opposite end of the room from the bar and plugged in their instruments. George Harrison and Jerry Garcia were on lead guitars; John Lennon was on rhythm guitar; Rick Danko was on base: I didn't recognise the drummer or the keyboard player.

'Wow, I don't believe this! What a band Jim!'

'Who is the other guitarist man?' asked Jim.

'You mean Jerry Garcia of the Grateful Dead.'

'Never heard of him either,' said Jim. 'And the bass player?'

'From a band called *The Band*. They were a great band.'

The bar quietened down while George and Jerry jammed for a while, with John Lennon adding a strong rhythm and Rick Danko and the drummer adding a driving beat. After three or four instrumental numbers, Elvis Presley strode onto the stage to a frisson of excitement, despite that fact that he has, according to Jim, being doing this gig for years, although not always with a band. Elvis looked great, dressed simply in blue jeans and a tight, white tee-shirt; he looked slim, fit and healthy. His thick head of hair had returned to its natural brown colour and was swept back from his forehead. The King looked magnificent.

The band kicked off with a medley of Beatles songs: *Can't Buy Me Love*, *Get Back*, *Lady Madonna* and *Drive my Car,* with John and Elvis taking turns on lead vocals, with George and Jerry on backing harmonies. The crowd in the bar were on their feet and immediately joined in and sang every line. There was a small space in front of the stage where men and women were dancing almost from the first bar of the first number. The band kept the tempo high with *Eight Days a Week*, *Ticket to Ride* and *We Can Work It Out* and for the next couple of hours the band and the King delighted everyone, the former were tight, as if they have been playing together for years, and the King was in fine voice on lead vocals for several Beatles numbers and a few of his own. After the first few songs, I felt the tears flow down my cheeks from the almost unbearable joy of the music. After each song, the crowd in the bar yelled their enthusiasm and my tears continued to flow and stung my eyes.

Song after song flowed into one another in a majestic symphony of Elvis and Beatles numbers. Elvis took the lead on most songs, with the rest of the band providing backing vocals or harmonies. The band romped through several more Beatles songs before they treated us to some of Elvis's best-known recordings, including *Always On My Mind*, *Mystery Train*, *Return to Sender* and *Love Letters*. He then took lead solo and sang George Harrison's *Something* and Paul

McCartney's *Yesterday* and slowed down the mood towards the end of the show.

The band then did *Here Comes the Sun*, followed by *The Sun KIng*, with John and Elvis in harmony before all too soon, it seemed, Elvis announced the last two songs: his own hit *Love Me Tender* and George's *All Things Must Pass* and then he and the band were gone. It was over, the most wonderful gig I have ever attended performed by a majestic band of musicians. The bar erupted with loud applause and cheers aimed at an empty stage and then fell silent for a few moments to let the realisation that the band had finished sink in.

Jim was beaming at me: 'Well, James, what did you think of that? Aren't you glad you came?'

'Oh, amazing Jim, just amazing. I never would have thought that I would hear Elvis singing *All Things Must Pass*. He sung it wonderfully. Do these guys play here often?'

'Yeah, not always the same band though. I've seen George Harrison and John Lennon play and sometimes Elvis shows up with an acoustic guitar and plays on his own or with Johnny Cash. I've seen Amy Winehouse duetting with Johnny Cash; that was great. There is usually some great music going on here from time to time. Aren't we the lucky ones eh? Let's have another drink before I take you back to your village.'

The level of noise in the bar rose several notches while last rounds of drinks were ordered and everyone seemed to be shouting at once after such a brilliant performance by Elvis and the band. It had been a *very* strange, unreal and exciting end to a day that left me frightened to wonder what would happen next and almost too fearful to contemplate whether there would be another day to be here in, wherever *here* is.

Chapter Three

Boz and the Creative Writing Group

It was dark when Jim dropped me at my house after the gig by Elvis and his band. The lights that glowed warmly from the houses on the green lent the village a welcoming and cosy air as I let myself in and waved to Jim as he roared off on his bike. I went upstairs immediately, lay fully clothed on one of the beds and fell asleep in a matter of seconds.

A strip of sunlight woke me: I must have fallen asleep without closing the curtains. My first thoughts were that I have woken up in a friend's house or in a hotel room, the usual feeling when in or, in this instance, *on* a strange bed, so that for several moments I looked up at the ceiling wondering where I was. Then I remembered: at least I had taken off the biker's leathers before I fell on the bed. My suit trousers looked very crumpled as did my shirt. One of the first things that I would do after breakfast is to have a shower and find a change of clothes.

I spent the next part of the morning setting about having a breakfast of scrambled eggs, toast and coffee, partly because I was hungry and partly to get used to some of the kitchen equipment. After breakfast, I had a shower and a change of clothes and went into the study. On one of the shelves on the back wall, I found several thick, hard-backed notebooks that contained lined pages of a very fine quality. I sat down at the large desk that was placed in the centre of the room, took up a pen from its silver holder and began to write a diary of yesterday's momentous events. I had not kept a diary in my previous life; I made an instant decision that I had to start now. It somehow seemed critically important that I recorded as much as possible about what had happened to me yesterday. I am not able to explain fully the urgency that I felt while sitting at the desk writing, but yesterday was such an amazing and puzzling day that I meant to write about it to satisfy myself that yesterday *had* happened: re-reading my diary entry would be proof of a sort, if proof were needed. Although this first diary entry might have been somewhat hurried, I closed the book when I was satisfied that I had recorded the events of the day.

Almost as soon as I closed the diary, I heard my smartphone ring and dashed around the ground floor of the house until I found it in the kitchen. I must have forgotten to switch it off when left it on the kitchen table sometime yesterday afternoon. The screen indicated that it is Kal.

'Good morning sir. How are you this morning? Have you found everything that you need for now?'

'Hello Kal. Yes, I'm fine thanks. I'm beginning to find my feet here. It is great to hear your voice Kal. As you can imagine, I felt rather odd and lonely when you left me to my own devices yesterday. I feel fine now.

'By the way, I started a diary this morning. I've never kept one before, but I thought that I needed some evidence about yesterday to convince myself about what happened to me. I've re-read it already this morning, just to ... I don't know ... to make sure.'

'A good idea sir. May I suggest that you try to write something each day. There is no harm in going into details about your first few days, they will make interesting reading in the future. After you have recorded your first impressions, you can always leave out the routine details and record other things. I'm sure that you are capable of deciding on these things. I will be round to see you in a few minutes. Is this convenient?'

'By all means Kal. How do I end a call by the way?'

'You just tap the screen anywhere and say "off" if you want to switch off your communicator.'

'Thanks Kal. Until later.' I ended the call and left my smartphone on the kitchen table.

※

I showed Kal into the study where I had been writing in the leather-bound notebook that I found earlier.

'Have you found everything that you need for your meals sir?' Kal settled himself in an armchair near the window.

'Thank you, yes. I am used to looking after myself. The house is well-equipped and well-stocked. Coffee? There's plenty. I found a brand-new cafétière in the kitchen this morning.'

'Thank you, no milk or sugar please. I know that you have been to the village shop, but I will explain how you replenish your supplies, go shopping and so forth, and other practical matters that are not dealt with by the local shop soon. Tell me about your writing?'

'I though that I would try to write down everything that happened during my first day here while it is still fresh in my mind. Last night was amazing. Jim took me to a bar out in a desert where an unbelievable band were playing. Just a moment, I'll get you a cup and saucer from the kitchen.'

'I thought that you would be impressed. So much better than an Elvis impersonation contest don't you think sir?' I handed Kal his coffee and returned to the table.

'I'm so glad that you have pre-empted my suggestion, so to speak. My main purpose in coming to see you this morning, apart from seeing how you are settling in of course, is to suggest that you keep a diary of your time here. It will come in useful later. I promise you.'

I am only vaguely convinced by the opaqueness of Kal's reason why I should keep a diary. I had already made up my mind to write everything down in the event that there might be a "later" of some sort. 'I'm not much of a writer,' I informed Kal, 'but I'd like to record my experience in this place as a narrative or memoir rather than a straightforward daily diary, or at least attempt to anyway. I think that a memoir will be more of a challenge that keeping a diary. I plan to keep a diary anyway, but translate it into a memoir at a later date, using the diary as an aid as it were.'

'I'm very pleased that you have said as much sir, I have just the thing for you. A certain Doctor Cynthia Maddox (of this parish) is the tutor for a creative writing class in the village hall. Her course starts again tomorrow evening. You will find regulars and some new members such as yourself. Don't be put off by the regulars. Most of them are very good writers but newcomers are made welcome. Would you like to try the course? It will help you to record your time here, help you to learn how to write ... lots of tips and so on. Thank you for the coffee.' Kal handed me his cup and saucer and a booklet. 'You will find all the details in there. The first of ten sessions is tomorrow evening. I feel certain that you will find the classes helpful and rewarding. I'll leave you to think it over. Doctor Maddox will be able to debit your fee - you pay in the way I showed you. I'll bid you good day sir. I will see myself out.'

'Bye Kal, thanks for this. I'll give the creative writing classes a go.'

I put my first tentative efforts at recording the events of yesterday to one side and perused the booklet. The course outline listed a number of themes that the course of classes undertakes to cover by discussion, in-class writing exercises, assignments and the study of professional novelists including characterisation, descriptive writing, and narration viewpoints. At first sight, this all seemed rather academic and theoretical but the booklet stressed that the various themes and topics would be explored by students completing a number of writing exercises and reading their work out to the group. *Reading out their work!* This phrase filled me with trepidation and echoed in my mind as I made my way across the village green to the hall the following evening.

※

A sizeable group of men and women were milling around inside the entrance to the village hall. A rather severe-looking, middle-aged woman detached herself from the small throng of would-be writers and introduced herself as 'Doctor Maddox, but please call me Cynthia. You are new, aren't you? We can sort out fees later. Please come and join the others.'

Cynthia clapped her hands in a mildly bossy fashion that was sufficient to round us up and ushered us into the hall. I began to feel nervous even before I had entered the room where I hoped to be enlightened about some of the mysteries of the writing process.

The hall smelled rather fusty but was bathed in a spectrum of light from the early evening sun emptying through stained glass windows at its far end, the effect of which countered the mustiness of our surroundings and lent it an air of temporary freshness. Chairs were arranged in the centre of the large hall in a semicircle in front of a single chair: Cynthia's chair, I presumed. It soon became clear who the regulars were by the confident manner in which they sat next to one another and chatted amiably: us newcomers merely took a seat and fiddled nervously with our notebooks.

Doctor Maddox took her seat. 'Good evening everyone and a very warm welcome to our regulars and especially to our newcomers. Some of you, of course, know one another but, for everyone's benefit, let us introduce ourselves starting at this end: just your name please.'

I counted twenty of us as the first member of the group introduced herself and as the appellations proceeded around the semicircle of chairs, past me somewhere in the middle until the other end was reached. (I wrote down all the names, about half and half men and women, most of whom were middle-aged in my estimation, with a few youngsters to make up the mix of folk attending tonight's class. If we all sit in different places next week, my diagram and list of names will be useless.)

'Thank you everyone and, again, let me welcome you, regulars and newcomers alike. Before we start this evenings class, I would just like to outline briefly some of the things that we will be covering during the course.' Doctor Maddox spent a few minutes expanding upon some of the material in the course booklet that Kal had given me. 'As you will see from the course outline,' she continued, 'there will be some structured sessions during the first half of the course and, in the second half of the course, I plan to spend most of the time on less structured tasks, get you to read out either your written work done for the course or extracts from whatever writing project you may be working on.

'I don't want *any* of you to feel under any pressure to read out your work. I have had plenty of students who have attended my courses and who have not read to us until week six or seven and several who have not read at all! Some students prefer to spend their time in this room listening to the work of others. So, and this is aimed in particular at our newcomers, listen, ask questions and - I hope - learn from the others and only read out when you feel that you are ready.' Doctor Maddox's outward appearance of apparent severity and frostiness gave way to an engaging smile as she opened her arms wide in a gesture of collective embrace.

Cynthia's reassurances had the desired affect on me: she wasn't as schoolmarmish as she appeared, I thought to myself, as my nervous state dissolved. At least I don't have to read out any of my work until I am good and ready, but read out *I will*.

The next part of the evening was spent in going round the room again so that members of the group could respond to Doctor Maddox's invitation to outline their current writing project. Most of the regulars and a few of the newcomers had something that they were working on, so I joined the group without a current writing project. I decided not to tell the group about my journal idea: 'They might think that writing about heaven is cliched,' Kal had quipped.

The remaining part of the evening, after a brief break for refreshments served at the back of the hall, was spent on an explanation of and a discussion about characterisation. Doctor Maddox outlined a number of parameters that the writer should consider when introducing and following the main character or characters in fiction. These included: physical description; personality; the notion that a character should be strongly drawn and be engaging; what motivates a character.   Doctor Maddox suggested that we should think about how these factors could work together so that the reader can *get to know the character*.

Although I had no plans to write any fiction, I hadn't been aware of the aspects of characterisation that we talked about during our first session. I was beginning to learn something already about the mechanics of writing, or so I thought, by the time the first class was over.

Doctor Maddox set us an assignment for the following week's session: to write a short piece that introduces a fictional character. 'For those of you who are already engaged on a project, you may bring something next week that you have already written. For our newcomers, perhaps you would like to try the task and next week let's hear what some of you have written. Think about our discussion of characterisation this evening.'

As soon as I returned home after class, I attempted the assignment. This is what I wrote.

> The first thing that anyone would notice about the old woman is her pronounced stoop over a shiny, red walking stick that appears to support her slight frame, both features, perhaps, signs of fragility or weakness. Or it is her hat that is noticed, broad-brimmed and intimidating? Suddenly, the old woman raises herself slightly and bellows 'I'll have that one!', raising her stick towards the largest television

screen in the store. The sound of the rubber ferule making contact with the pristine screen freezes nearby shoppers and the woman's attendant salesman into an alarmed silence.

'Be careful Mother', whispers the anxious-looking, middle-aged man who accompanies the old woman.

'I'm only explaining which one I want', she retorts loudly.

This exchange breaks the silence, if not the TV screen, and the salesman, previously rooted to the spot with horror, regains his composure. 'Certainly madam, do you have a Nectar card?'

Now I see her as a young woman, tall, straight and strong of limb and will, carrying two pails of milk suspended from a wooden frame across her slender shoulders, a determined look on her face, the same look that I see now as she looks up at me. 'What the hell is a Nectar card?' she demands.

Most of the next session, in the following week, was taken up with members of the group reading aloud what they had written for the first assignment. The essays in characterisation were vibrant and skilfully written and promoted much praise and discussion amongst members of the group, with Doctor Maddox injecting honest and useful criticism from time to time. Any negative comments offered by either Doctor Maddox or a member of the group were put forward warmly and gently so as not to offend new members and were given in a spirit of encouragement. Even so, it was noticeable that some of the regulars were a little harder on each other than they were on newcomers.

After we had listened and commented on a few offerings, Doctor Maddox turned to me: 'How about you James? Would you like to read aloud; I know it's only the second session?'

'Er ... okay, here goes,' I said after recovering from the slight shock of Doctor Maddox remembering my name and singling me out.

'I didn't mean to press you unduly; I merely meant to enquire if you had tackled last week's assignment.'

'Will I be kept in if I haven't done it Miss?' This very feeble attempt at comedy raised a few smiles and a chuckle from Cynthia. 'Sorry, I bet you've heard that one before.'

'Oh, just a few times James, but, no matter, the old ones are the best ones. Would you like to ...?'

'Yep, I'll read what I have written, but can I tell you and the group that I haven't done anything like this before and it is going to be scary. It's not actually a fictional characterisation. It's based loosely on an incident that happened when I took my mother shopping to a superstore, the kind of massive place that sells everything from food to electrical goods. I've exaggerated and tinkered around with the actual incident. I'd be glad to know what you think.' I cast a quick glance around the hall, cleared my throat and read what I had written after last week's session.

Most of the comments that followed my reading were, to my delight, very positive. There had even been some laughter during my reading of my brief piece. 'Very good James,' Cynthia said, 'a very brave first attempt at something creative and very brave of you to read aloud so soon into the course; well done. I liked the way you changed the point of view at the end. We will talk about that next week.

Let's move on to someone else. Harry?'

'I didn't really know what I was doing with the switch at the end Cynthia; it just came out that way. Sorry Harry, I didn't mean to interrupt your piece.'

'That's okay James,' said Harry, 'your mum sounds like a feisty woman.'

As the remainder of the evening progressed, I sat back, relaxed and allowed myself to feel a little bit pleased with myself. It will be tougher next time, I thought to myself; they will give me a hard time next time.

Towards the end of the second session, Cynthia confirmed that the theme of next week's session would centre on narrative viewpoints. 'We will explore examples of multiple viewpoints - remember what James did at the end of his piece. However, before we finish for this evening, I have an exciting announcement to make.' Cynthia waited for us to cease putting our notebooks and other things away until the room fell silent and we were alert with expectation. 'Mister Charles Dickens will be honouring us with his presence during next week's session.'

A chorus of exclamations burst from the group until it seemed that everyone was babbling hastily at once. Cynthia was forced to clap her hands loudly to quieten the room. 'I am sure that you will all agree that we are most privileged to be receiving a visit from such a famous novelist. Mister Dickens will be reading to us and I believe that he will take questions. There won't be time for all of us to ask a question, but more of that next week. Until next week then.'

The hubbub continued until we had left the village hall and had gathered outside in the dusk of mid-evening. Instead of dispersing for home, the members of Doctor Maddox's creative writing group lingered on the village green contemplating the enormity of the fact that one of the most well-known writers ever to have lived would be visiting our group next week. Cynthia had said that during the course we would be studying the work of professional writers, but she had given no indication that we would actually meet someone of the stature of Charles Dickens. Eventually, we bade each other goodnight in a mood of suppressed anticipation for what was to come next week.

※

'Mister Dickens is due to arrive soon,' said Cynthia at the start of the next class. 'He doesn't usually take questions, but I've managed to persuade him to answer just a few questions after he has read to us. I'm sure that we all have questions that we would like to ask, but we couldn't possibly ask our guest to answer twenty or so questions. So, to make it fair I've put all of your names into a hat - well, a cardboard box actually - and, shall we say, the first six names drawn can ask a question. Does this meet with everyone's approval?'

There followed a general murmur of ascent as Cynthia asked Sylvia, who usually sat at one end of the semicircle of chairs, to draw out six folded pieces of paper and hand them to Cynthia.

'Before I read out the names, may I set out some ground rules. Mister Dickens has stipulated that we may ask only questions about literature, in other words please don't ask him questions about his former family, his former personal life, relationships and so forth. Please stick to literary questions. I feel sure that you will appreciate and accord with his wishes.' Again, a chorus of approval followed Cynthia's appeal.

'After all,' said Harry, 'this is a writing group, we should respect his wishes. It's a great privilege to have him here. In his former life, he read to large audiences. You must have a lot of influence Cynthia.'

Cynthia merely smiled at Harry's observation and read out six names, including mine. I had already thought of a question and even though I hadn't read a great deal of Dickens, I hoped that my relative unfamiliarity with his work would not show me up in the company of my fellow students.

'If you would excuse me,' said Cynthia, 'Mister Dickens should be here very soon.' Cynthia moved her chair to join Sylvia's end of the semicircle and motioned to me. 'James, would you pull the lectern forward and place it about here. Mind the jug of water. We mustn't forget that Mister Dickens does not permit anyone to sit behind him; he never liked this when he gave his very many readings.' Cynthia seemed satisfied with the seating arrangements and left the hall.

We could hear voices in the entrance to the village hall before Cynthia entered the hall accompanied by an immediately recognisable figure. Here was one of the most well-known nineteenth century novelists of our former lives, celebrated widely in the United Kingdom and in the United States of America. Every schoolchild in the post-Victorian era should have heard of Charles Dickens, even if they had not read any of his novels or had not seen any of the numerous television or film adaptations of them. Here, before us, in our village hall, was one of the foremost chroniclers of the Victorian age; its education and its law and social reform were amongst the sphere of his interest and concern within and without his storytelling. Here is the man of whom Karl Marx had said "... [he] issued to the world more political and social truths that have been uttered by all [of] the professional politicians, publicists and moralists put together."

All eyes followed the slightly-built man that accompanied Cynthia to the lectern. There was the impressive, pointed beard, the unruly, flyaway greying hair and broad, high forehead that I had seen in photographic plates inserted into biographies of the novelist. His complexion was darker than I imagined from black and white photographs and his overall appearance in a long velvet-trimmed coat lent him an expected old-fashioned guise that, nevertheless, did not detract from an immediate sense of authority and confidence that was palpable as he took his place behind the lectern.

Charles Dickens placed his hands on the sides of the lectern and waited for Cynthia to speak. His coat was unbuttoned and splayed out sufficiently to reveal a high wing collar, a tie with a clasp, white shirt and a high-buttoned, dark green waistcoat that sported a pocket watch.

The village hall was in complete silence as Cynthia introduced our esteemed guest. 'Ladies and gentlemen, our humble writing group has the honour, this evening, of welcoming a very special guest. As you know, part of the course includes a study of the work of professional writers to help inform our amateur efforts. What better way to do this than in the presence of one of the most eminent writers of what we referred to in our former lives as the nineteenth century or of *any* century, in my view. Mister Dickens has kindly offered to read us some extracts from his novels and will be glad to answer a few questions later. Mister Charles Dickens.' Cynthia took her seat and Charles Dickens took a sip of water, cleared his throat delicately, opened a book and met our gaze with his.

'Thank you Cynthia,' the great man began, 'it gives me great pleasure to be with you this evening.' His voice was strong and confident, if not a little husky and low which masked a more powerful mode of speech that must have been evident in the public performances of his readings. 'I would like to read three extracts from *Great Expectations*.'

It was, initially, something of a shock to experience the theatrical manner of Dickens reading his own work. By modern standards, his performance might be interpreted as melodramatic or, in modern vernacular, 'over the top'. After a few minutes though, we were soon taken in by the sheer power of his reading which was amplified by hand and arm gestures and by the force of the gaze of his rather large eyes when he frequently looked up from his copy of *Great Expectations* and completed sentences without returning to the page. I could only assume that the reason why Dickens had taken acting lessons during his previous life was so that he could enhance his performance when reading to an audience. It was Annie Thackeray, daughter of William Makepeace Thackeray, the novelist and contemporary of Charles Dickens, who observed that Dickens created "a sort of brilliance in [a] room, mysteriously dominant and formless. I remember how everyone lighted up when he entered." We were immediately under the spell of Dickens's power and dominance of us, his audience.

It also soon became clear that Charles Dickens was in possession of an extraordinary ability to give a distinctive voice to each of his characters: to the narrator, to the main character Pip when in conversation with other characters, to his sister and her husband Joe and, spectacularly, to the convict Magwitch who Pip, as a young boy, encounters very near the beginning of the novel. (*Hook the reader early*, I rapidly scribbled in my notebook. I didn't want to spend much time looking down at my notebook, but the encounter with Magwitch is absolutely key to the story of Pip.)

Dickens rendered the voice of Magwitch with such terrifying conviction that it chilled the blood. The village hall seemed to darken during the reading of the first extract due to the presence of Magwitch and the fear that he implanted into the young boy, a fear that seemed to extend to us, his audience.

'Some of you might remember, if you have read *Great Expectations*, what happens to Pip when he has grown up a little,' Dickens was saying. 'He was sent to play at Miss Havisham's crumbling manor house and be humiliated by her alluring ward Estella. This is how it happens.'

Charles Dickens then led us, with the hapless Pip, on his first visit to Miss Havisham. We could feel Pip's anxiety and his immediate fascination with the beautiful Estella and his apprehension in the presence of Miss Havisham and her decrepit surroundings. Dickens's vivid account of Pip's first encounter with the old woman and the young girl left us in no doubt that Miss Havisham and Estella have crucial parts to play in Pip's life. Although I had read *Great Expectations* a long time ago, Dickens's reading of Pip's encounter with Magwitch, Miss Havisham and Estella served as a reminder that the book is a great work of literary fiction.

'For those of you who have read *Great Expectations*, you will have read the *alternative* ending. The ending that was published is different to my original ending. Finally, I would like to finish by reading my original ending. Perhaps you would like to compare it with the published ending.' Dickens glanced towards Cynthia.

Dickens did not elaborate on the exact reason why there were two endings to *Great Expectations* and it was evident from the murmured reaction to his introduction to the evening's final reading that most of us were unaware that there were two endings: I certainly was.

'We will make that an exercise for next week's class: thank you for the suggestion Mister Dickens.'

'I've noticed that a number of film makers manage to change the ending by making it even more optimistic than I was persuaded to do so in the published novel. As a consequence of the change from my original ending, no-one has made a film that captured what I had written originally. *This* is what I intended in my original ending: an affirmation of parting and unrequited love. Pip and Estella do not spend the rest of their lives together, as suggested by some of the film and television adaptations, or - as some have suggested - as implied by the published ending. What I wanted to convey to the reader was the sense of a final understanding between our two characters, Pip and Estella, an understanding that their lives had grown apart, that Pip could not be with Estella but that finally she understood - against all of Miss Havisham's "teachings" - what was in Pip's heart. This is what I wrote for the original ending.'

Charles Dickens finished his performance by reading, in a soft, low voice that was tinged with sadness his account of the final, fortuitous meeting between Pip and Estella, as the narrator led us towards the end of their story.

We accompanied Pip as Estella's servant runs after him in the street and escorts him to Estella's carriage that happens to be passing. Our two protagonists exchange pleasantries and part. I imagined Pip watching the carriage move away, his emotions in turmoil but, perhaps, left with an undying and undeniable feeling that Estella finally understood what Pip's love meant to them both but was never fulfilled.

The impact of the original ending of the novel was felt by all of us as Charles Dickens closed his copy of *Great Expectations* and we burst into enthusiastic and prolonged applause. Eventually he held up his hands in a gesture of supplication.

'That was wonderful Mister Dickens,' said Cynthia. 'Will you have time for a few questions?' Charles Dickens nods in agreement. 'James, you first.'

'Mister Dickens,' I began, 'thank you so much for illuminating us about some of the themes of *Great Expectations*. I didn't know about your first ending and I agree with you: most film makers meddle with the published ending unnecessarily. My question concerns *Bleak House*. Our group is studying points of view in fiction. I wonder if you were the first author to adopt *multiple* points of view. For instance, in Chapter Three, the point of view suddenly changes from that of the narrator to Esther's narrative in the first person. Why did you write *Bleak House* in this way rather from a single narrator's viewpoint? In other words, what led you to invent multiple points of view?'

'A very good question sir. I'm uncertain whether I invented this technique, as you put it; I certainly was unaware of any of my English contemporaries using the technique, although there may well have been authors in Europe who made use of this feature of style, unbeknown to me at the time.

'In essence, I tried it out because the novel to which you refer is long. The technique of using more than one narrator is, in my view, likely to work only in a long novel that contains many characters. Whilst Esther Summerson is, of course, the central character, she is surrounded by many other characters who have a bearing on her story. Therefore, one can invite the reader to follow the plot from the point of view of more than one character. At the same time that the narrator moves the plot along from an *external* point of view, Esther's narrative is meant to draw you in from *her* point of view.

'Remember that in my time, novels were often published in episodes or instalments. Thus, I could easily switch points of view from one chapter to another, from instalment to instalment if necessary. The important thing is not to lose or confuse your reader when you change from one point of view to another. You can signal to the reader that the point of view is changing. Does this answer your question?'

'Yes, thank you Mister Dickens: a very interesting answer.'

Cynthia cued the other members of the group who were going to ask questions, all of which Charles Dickens answered effusively. We learnt that his experience as a lawyer's clerk led to the comic or sinister depiction of lawyers and their profession in a number of his novels and he talked about his concern for institutions such as education and prisons and how he gave voice to them in his fiction. He also talked about childhood and its importance as a theme in his novels and he mentioned how he found it difficult to write strong female characters. 'Perhaps this is the lot of us male writers; how can we really know anything about the fairer, stronger sex? All that we can do is use our imagination and help our readers see a story through the eyes of our characters.

'My advice to all of you is: try to make your characters strong; your readers should be allowed to get to know your characters, in particular your main character. May I wish all of you the very best of good fortune in your writing endeavours.'

'Thank you,' we chorussed, and applauded again as Cynthia escorted the great man out of the hall.

❊

The air of excitement continued until the next session of the writing group when we discussed the relative merits of the two endings to *Great Expectations* and we commented on what Dickens had to say about multiple points of view. We didn't come to a consensus about the two endings of the novel. About half of the group preferred the sadder, pessimistic ending - the one that Dickens had read to us -and the other half preferred the slightly optimistic ending - the one that was published - where Dickens suggests, rather obliquely, that Pip and Estella will not part again. Without intending to sound deliberately obtuse or provocative, I suggested that Dickens could have ended the published novel *before* Pip and Estella meet for the final time, in other words Pip and Estella never meet again after they had gone their separate ways earlier in the novel.

'A pity that you didn't ask him that,' said Cynthia. 'I wonder what his response would have been?'

'I'm not sure that I would have had the courage to suggest a third ending. Besides, I had already drawn lots to ask one question; I wouldn't have been fair to ask another one.'

'And a very good question it was James, as were all of the questions that you all asked last week. Wasn't it interesting to hear the views of the author who probably invented the technique of multiple points of view? Let's remind ourselves about James's story about his mother buying a television. You changed the point of view from the narrator to the first person at the end of the piece. Why did you do that James?'

'Er ... the idea just came to me when I was writing the piece on characterisation. I know what I wanted to do at the time, but I didn't know *what* I was doing, technically I mean.'

'Well, I think that it worked,' said Cynthia. 'What does the group think?'

There followed a lengthy discussion about multiple points of view, before Cynthia left us with the homework task of identifying other authors from our former lives who have used this technique in fiction so that we could explore its effectiveness in context.

※

As I write this part of my memoir, I cannot leave the account of the creative writing group without expressing admiration for our tutor, Cynthia, in the way she encouraged us and proffered praise and constructive criticism of our efforts. As I reflect on my fellow group members, I am left with a feeling of admiration for the pieces of writing that they read aloud. Most of the work of my contemporaries was enticing, enthralling and was written brilliantly. I usually felt out of my depth compared to such fascinating pieces of science fiction, family history, war and crime stories and so on. One elderly woman, Kathy, read us wonderful short stories. One story about two elderly men reflecting upon their childhoods evoked a spontaneous round of applause.

Cynthia usually used the second half of each session, after we had explored the evening's topic, whether it be characterisation, dialogue, descriptive writing or some other specific topic, to hear what we had written as a result of the previous session. Thus I heard lots of examples of the skill of my fellow members and I even plucked up the courage to read aloud twice more before the course ended.

My second reading, which I won't include in this memoir, was less successful than my first effort. Good dialogue but poor descriptive work was the general view of the group. The negative criticism dented what little confidence that I had gained, pierced my psyche so that I felt a pang of disappointment. 'Don't worry about it,' Kal had said. 'I'm sure that you will improve with practice. Remember why you are attending this course. It's not a competition. What is the next assignment about?'

'As it happens, descriptive writing,' I told Kal when I returned home after the session when I read aloud for the second time. 'We've tackled this theme before, but Cynthia says that we should be able to improve the descriptive element of our work by bringing what we have learnt so far to bear: "give it impact" is what she said. She said that we can write about an event, a visit, anything really: anything that has plenty of scope of *describing* surroundings, feelings and so on. We can still have dialogue, but Cynthia suggested that we keep it to a minimum so that we can exercise our descriptive skills.'

'There we are then sir, now's your chance to put dialogue to one side to some extent - you say that you have received good feedback for that - and concentrate on painting strong images in a descriptive piece of writing.'

'Oh I like your notion of "painting images" Kal,' I said. 'You sound quite the expert.'

Following my less than well-received second reading, I had asked Cynthia if she would put my name down to read the following week. 'I want to see if I can improve my descriptive writing,' I told her at the next session.

'Of course James, I'll call on your first next week. We don't have a specific topic for next week's session, so I think that we will spend the whole evening hearing what members of the group have been writing recently.'

I was the first to read aloud in the next session. My third piece was quite well received in that members of the group said that I had improved since my second reading to the extent that they could "see" the scenes painted in the following words.

> Several years ago in my former life I got involved in a research project that investigated the eye condition that I suffer from, a condition known as congenital nystagmus. I soon became friendly with Josephine, the leader of the project, as a result of regular visits to her research laboratory that was located in one of London's teaching hospitals. I was more than willing to volunteer as Josephine was having difficulty finding enough people with the condition for her experimental work. A typical visit would last no more than a hour or two and usually required me to take a day off from work so that I could travel up to London for the day. One such visit to Josephine's

laboratory stands out more than any of the others: the day that Nelson Mandela spoke to the crowd in Trafalgar Square in the centre of London.

The day had dawned bright and springlike as I took the train to London. One of Josephine's research students carried out a number of exhaustive tests that demanded all of my powers of concentration, some of which he was forced to repeat so that he could gain consistent results. Eventually I was allowed to escape the darkened laboratory after bidding goodbye to Josephine (until the next time) and emerged blinking and weary into the early spring light of a late morning in London. On the way to Josephine's laboratory, I had heard on the taxi driver's radio that Nelson Mandela was in London and that it was possible that he might appear on the balcony of South Africa House, overlooking Trafalgar Square. I already knew, from listening to the news on the radio in the days leading up to his visit, that Mister Mandela was in London but I didn't know what his itinerary was and it wasn't until I left the hospital that the thought crossed my mind that I ought to go to Trafalgar Square on the off-chance that something might be happening. For all I knew, cooped up in the laboratory for most of the morning, I could easily have missed catching sight of Nelson Mandela. I was in this casual frame of mind as I found the nearest underground train station, studied the map and worked out a route to Trafalgar Square.

After a few stops and one change, I left the underground network at Leicester Square and made for the north-east corner of Trafalgar Square. I don't know why I thought that there might be a small crowd, but what I saw surpassed my modest expectations. As I emerged into the square, I found myself on the edge of a vast crowd. The palpable air of expectation suggested that whatever the crowd was waiting for had not happened yet and, almost by happenstance, I was in time. Traffic had been stopped on the north and west sides of the square and the square itself was absolutely packed with people with one thought in mind: to catch a glimpse of one of the most famous and admired men in the world.

I decided that I would have to make an effort to make inroads into the crowd so that I could be nearer to the front of South Africa house. My original position near the entrance to the National Gallery on the north side of the square was too far away so I gradually and gently pushed my way into the mass of people. After careful progress, I secured a position that was quite a long way from the edge of the crowd and about seventy metres from the front of South Africa House. My immediate neighbours in the crowd assured me that Nelson Mandela had been seen arriving some minutes earlier and he had been seen going inside South Africa House and would be appearing on the balcony soon. I don't know how they knew this: I didn't question this apparent fact, but its revelation filled me with as much excitement and anticipation as those standing near to me were clearly feeling.

How different was this scene from the days when Trafalgar Square was host to demonstrations against the apartheid regime in South Africa. Now the country is free from apartheid and its most famous advocate of a free South Africa was about to step out onto the balcony that in the past would have born witness to the noise and rhetoric of anti-apartheid demonstrations but that now overlooked a display of a quite different emotion. Now all that the crowd wanted was the man himself: the time for demonstrating was long past.

We spent what seemed like an age looking up at the balcony, watching for the slightest movement. The sun burned our faces and the chatter and banter was loud and amicable. I stood in the sun watching and waiting, drawn into the collective emotion of the crowd, bonding with those around me in the knowledge that we were as one, waiting for our hero.

Then, suddenly, the people at the front let out an enormous roar that flowed swiftly backwards as the remainder of the crowd saw what they saw: there was movement on the balcony. The noise died down momentarily as the mass of people in the square seemed to act as an organic whole, trying to determine what was happening. Just as soon as the volume of noise subsided, a figure moved to the front of the balcony and started to speak. The cheer that was sent up into the cloudless sky above the centre of London was a joy to be part of; it went on and on and was refreshed and amplified every few seconds by another section of the huge crowd so that it echoed and re-echoed from the buildings that surround Trafalgar Square. Admiral Nelson, from his position on the top of his column in the centre of the square, must have wondered what manner of man was this *other* Nelson who could ignite the wave of admiration and emotion that began far below his lonely vantage point and swept upwards past him to fade into the ether.

Nelson Mandela waited and raised his hand in an attempt to calm us down and started his speech again. 'I would like to take you home in my pocket ...' is as far as he got when another massive cheer leapt from the crowd in response to these opening words. I could feel the sheer, collective love that flowed from the crowd, aimed at the diminutive man in a flowery shirt whose silver hair seemed to shimmer in the shadow of the building to make him visible to all corners of the square as he spoke to us. A young, white South African standing next to me turned to me and said: 'That's my president ... that's *my* president.' The tears running down his cheeks pushed me easily across the border between feeling near to tears and letting them flow.

After what seemed like only a few short minutes, Nelson Mandela thanked the citizens of the United Kingdom for their support while South Africa was fighting for its freedom and then he was gone. The crowd was stunned into silence and waited pointlessly to see if he would reappear. We soon realised that we had been graced by the presence of a great and humble man and I felt very lucky to have been standing in Trafalgar Square on that spring day in London. The square began to empty and its occupants drifted away to return to their lives and carried with them the memory of a few short minutes in the presence of a genuine hero of our times.

Some years later, I heard a journalist on the World Service of the British Broadcasting Corporation say to Nelson Mandela that one criticism that has been levelled at him is that he has always sought to find and believe the good in people. 'There is an element of truth in that,' was his brief reply. The same criticism has also been written of another of my heroes, namely Anne Frank. She was a prisoner, like Nelson Mandela, also confined as one facing brutal oppression and intolerance. Nelson Mandela and Anne Frank are divided by many years in age and time and are separated by gender and country but they have at least one thing in common, they both saw the good in people, despite the fact that Nelson Mandela spent twenty seven years of his life in prison for his beliefs and that Anne Frank paid for hers with her life and the life of most of her family.

At the end of the session Cynthia asked me if she could pass my piece of writing to someone; she didn't say who. 'I know someone who would like to read your piece James; may I have this copy?'

'Of course,' I said. 'Who is it for?'

'Just ... someone,' said Cynthia, 'an interested party one might say.'

'Oh, very mysterious Cynthia. I don't mind.'

I thought little more of Cynthia's "interested party" until, a few days later, Kal - on one of his regular visits - said: 'Some very important people would like to meet you. This family don't permit many visitors. They lead a very private, secluded and protected life. Would you like me to make the necessary arrangements?'

Little did I know what an impact the invitation that Kal had conveyed would have on me when the identity of Cynthia's mysterious 'someone' was revealed.

Chapter Four

The Painter in the Garden

George Harrison's garden looked a delight the day I met the painter. Shrubs and flowers bulged and blazed with colour and scent as I wandered along familiar paths that weaved their gravelly way through the woods and along the shores of lakes in this wonderful garden. On the many times that I have visited the garden, I have occasionally happened across one of George's team of gardeners working intently on some solitary task. Other than the official gardeners, I rarely meet anyone else in the garden, although I have often noticed a young woman in the summerhouse by the larger of the two lakes. Her head is usually bent forward, as if she is reading or writing. I have only noticed her from a distance, never at the instant when she must look up from her work from time to time.

    On the odd occasion that I came across George, he was usually to be seen kneeling in front of a border, tending plants in the mysterious way that gardeners do, always finding something that needs to be done. As for me, a dedicated, non-gardener who can hardly name a single plant, flower or tree, I feel privileged to be allowed to enter, wander and enjoy the beauty, harmony and serenity of George's garden.

    Kal had arranged it so that I could enter the garden. 'All is arranged sir,' he said one day shortly after my arrival. If you follow my directions - it will take you about an hour to walk there, down the valley - you will come across a door in a hedge marked *Strictly Private*. Don't be put off: you have permission to enter via this entrance.' I resisted asking Kal about the disturbing dream that I had last night and followed his directions.

George's garden comprises two lakes, one larger than the other, with a waterfall and oriental bridge at the point where the larger lake flows into the smaller one. Ferns and rock gardens slope up from the water's edge of both lakes and flowers float on their surface. Tall, blue fir trees flank the shores and create several woodland walks through Japanese gardens and other themed garden rooms.

On the day I met the painter, I had seen George pruning a tall bush that was awash with orange flowers. I was about to turn around and avoid bothering him when he gestured to me to approach him. 'There's someone over there that I think you'd like to meet; he won't mind chatting while he is working,' George said quietly, as if not to disturb the figure he was pointing towards with his secateurs.

'Does he work for you here?' I asked George in a low voice.

'No, no. He comes here to paint. Its great that he regards my garden as suitable subject matter.'

'Surely painters don't like to be disturbed though,' I said hesitantly.

'It'll be okay, you'll see.   Go on over.' George gestured again with his pruning shears and went back to work on the bush.

I could see the painter's back from where I was standing. He was clad in a shabby, heavy brown jacket in spite of the mid-morning heat and was sitting on a rickety chair in a way that made it appear that he has to lean a long way forward to work on his canvas that is, I imagined from this distance, propped up on an equally rickety easel.

I crossed the broad expanse of lawn between the path and the painter and approached the figure bent intently towards his work. The painter couldn't have seen me but he must have heard my faint footsteps swish through the grass. 'You can sit next to me on the grass if you like; I don't think that it will still be damp by this time in the morning.' He spoke without a pause between rapid brush stokes and without casting a glance in my direction.

'Thank you. I didn't want to disturb you at your work but George said ... '

'He is a good and gentle man; he loves nature as I do.' The painter turned and looked down at me with a slightly unnerving intensity. I recognised him immediately. 'I am trying to capture the shape and colour of those irises that George has planted down there.   His garden is very fine, don't you think?'   The intense gaze continued as I detect a slight Dutch accent on "don't you think?".

The edge of the lawn beyond where we were sitting dips down slightly towards a display of purple irises interspersed with tall, wispy, yellow grasses. The smaller of the garden's two lakes lies beyond and further still, in the middle distance, low hills rise above the tranquil valley that embraces George's garden.

'I knew that you are English because I heard you speaking to George. I hope that my English is good. I leant to speak it before I came to England to teach for a time in Ramsgate.'

'Perfect,' I ventured. I studied the profile of the man who brought so much pleasure to millions of people in the many decades after his death. 'Have you any idea what your paintings mean to so many people ... in our former place, as it were?'

'I have heard much talk of it,' he replied. 'It didn't happen in my lifetime but I am glad that my work was appreciated after my death.'

Vincent van Gogh continued to apply thick dabs of paint to his half-finished canvas. The blues and purples of the irises merged and pulsated and the shades of green of the stems and leaves seemed to vibrate with freshness and solidity. I have gazed in wonder at similar paintings of flowers in the leading art galleries of my former world, but watching one being made is thrilling almost beyond description. Vincent's command of the juxtaposition of colours took place vividly and rapidly before my unbelieving eyes.

'We will meet again soon.' I took this to be a mild hint that I should leave Vincent to continue to paint in peace.

'Au revoir, monsieur,' I said as I get up from the grass.

'Au revoir; a bientôt,' Vincent replied as I stole a final look at the work in progress and made my way back across the lawn to the path.

※

A few days later, I happened across Vincent again. He was working at the boundary edge of George's garden at a place where a grassy bank gently slopes away into a shallow valley of small fields and clusters of trees.

'A landscape this time?' I ventured.

'I like the combination of the colours and textures down there. What do you think?'

I was standing behind Vincent's left shoulder as he worked quickly on what I took to be an almost finished work. The slabs of paint representing the fields below us harmonised perfectly with the vivid green of the trees. The sky was dense with turquoise and the yellow sun swirled at the top the painting. There was a rhythm and energy throughout the work that brought the placid landscape to a dazzling intensity. And Vincent van Gogh was asking *me* what *I* think.

'It's wonderful, Mister van Gogh. It's absolutely wonderful.'

'Please call me Vincent.' He turned to look at me with his penetrating gaze. 'I am so glad you like it. When I am out here, I often can finish a painting in one day.'

It was early evening; he had probably been here all day. I sat on the bank next to him, taking care not to disturb the paint-stained, canvas bag with its tubes, brushes and a spare palette that was spilling out onto the grass near his feet.

'Would you pass me that rag, the one just inside the bag. Thank you, it will save me having to put the palette on the grass again.'

I found the rag and passed it up to him. He gripped his paint brush between his teeth and took the rag in his right hand so that he could dab at one corner of his painting. He leant back in his rickety chair, satisfied, and handed the rag back to me without a word. I was now Vincent's assistant.

Vincent went back to work on the offending corner with one of the several paint brushes that were held between the fingers of his left hand, the hand that supported his colour palette. The fingers of both of his hands were stained with brightly-coloured paint that he squeezed onto his palette from white tubes that I found in his bag and passed to him when requested. My mundane help saved him bending down and searching amongst the contents of his bag. I was beginning to get the hang of my new role as assistant to the great painter.

'George brought me some bread and cheese and a pitcher of cold water a few hours ago. Such a kind man.'

'He is very much missed,' I replied. 'Many, many people missed George when he died a few years ago. To some, he was their favourite Beatle.'

'Ah, the Beatles. George and his friends were famous, I am told.'

'Famous ... I'll say! So were you. Have you any idea how much this painting would sell for? Millions, very many millions, that's what, back there ... you know, where we used to be.

It is only very wealthy people and possibly some art galleries that could afford a van Gogh. We're talking tens of millions of dollars or pounds here. If I had the money - which, of course, I don't - I would ask you if this one is for sale.'

'It's yours, you can have this one when it is finished. It's very nearly finished.' Vincent's usually serious expression broke into a broad smile.

'*I* can't afford it Vincent. It's out of the question. I haven't quite yet worked out how money works in this community; it's a mystery, much like everything else that has happened to me since my recent arrival. If there is one thing that I am certain of though, it is that there is no possible way that I could afford to buy a Vincent van Gogh painting: that's for sure.'

The smile hadn't left his face. 'No, it's not for sale. I mean that you can have it ... it's yours.'

I am unable to speak for a few moments while I try to take in the enormity of what Vincent has said to me. 'You mean that you are prepared to spend all this time on a painting only to give it away to someone that you hardly know. No ... I couldn't accept your incredible offer, I couldn't possibly accept.'

'And why not? You obviously liked my work before you arrived here; you told me as much. I am satisfied with today's work and I wish you to have it. Please ... I insist.'

'Mr. Vincent, Vincent I mean, how can I ever thank you. I must be dreaming.'

'This place is made for dreams isn't it? What is your Guardian's name? I will arrange for the painting to be delivered to your house. When the canvas is completely dry, I will sign and frame it and arrange for it to be send to you.'

Vincent got up from his chair and busied himself with packing up his rickety gear. The palettes were stowed in his bag, facing each other so that the unused paint didn't get everywhere, tops of tubes were replaced and paint brushes were wiped with well-used rags and put away. My services as assistant weren't called upon during these activities.

I hesitated to bring up the topic, but decided to mention it anyway. 'By way of thanks though and if I had the chance, I know exactly where I would donate this painting. It would be to the Vincent van Gogh centre in Auvers-sur-Oise. There is a ready-made space on the wall of your garret, waiting for one of your paintings to be hung. The centre can't afford an original of course. If only there was some way that I could give them this one. Even if I could, it would cause a mighty rumpus in the art world as there would be no record that you had painted this one in your lifetime. Wouldn't it be fun to watch the experts argue over its authenticity?'

'You have been to Auvers?' Vincent paused during his much-practiced gear-stowing routine. The finished painting was wrapped in a large cloth that must have been stored in the bottom of his bag. The chair and easel were collapsed and joined the wrapped canvas in a flat arrangement that Vincent strapped together. Everything else was stowed in the ancient, brown canvas bag.

'I carry this on my back and the bag on my shoulder,' he explained. 'Tell me about Auvers. As you seem to know, I lived there for a time. I spent my last few months there.' Vincent carefully laid his gear on the grass and sat next to me. We sat side by side at the top of the grassy bank that leads down into the valley that has been the subject of Vincent's thoughts and emotions for the day. The soft evening light lent a sublime tranquility to the landscape in front of us and there was enough warmth in the sinking sun to delay the promise of the chill to come. 'I would like to hear about Auvers.'

'Well, it's probably much larger than when you lived there. It is more strung out along the road to Pontoise. You would probably recognise the centre of the village though. The little church that you painted is still there, of course, and the mayor's house and they have kept the cafe as it was in your day, the one opposite the mayor's house. In fact, the cafe is at the front of the Vincent van Gogh centre. The village really took you to its heart after you died. At the rear of the cafe is a shop that sells all kinds of things, such as calendars, books and so on, all kinds of stuff that is connected to you and your paintings. You can go upstairs, above the shop, and have a look at your room. If I remember rightly, it is a bare room, save for a bed and a chair I think. It is quite a few years since I visited, so I could be wrong about the furniture. Anyway, I do remember the space on the wall that I told you about. It is as if it is waiting for one of your paintings to be hung. The centre cannot afford the several tens of millions of pounds that it would take to purchase one of your paintings on the rare occasion that one comes up on the open market, but the space is there waiting to be filled.

'People come and visit Auvers from all over the world. There were some Japanese tourists there the day that I visited. A few followed me to the edge of the field on the plateau above the village where you painted the wheat field with crows. It was one of my favourite walks, from the church up to the plateau.'

'Mine too,' said Vincent, 'but you can probably tell that from my paintings from that part of the village.'

'What they have done, in the village,' I continued, 'is to place a weather-proof copy of a number of your paintings on to a kind of horizontal board, about waist high so that anyone can stand on the spot where you painted the picture and look at the copy. There are several of these boards dotted around the village and you can get a map of where they are from the van Gogh centre and take a walking tour around the village and study the paintings where you made them. It's a great idea. This is what tourists to the village do; they come because of you and your work. It is quite a famous place.'

'I also visited Doctor Gachet's house. I was the only visitor. Quite a small house; interesting though. And, if I remember rightly, he had a herb garden.'

'A fine man. He helped me a great deal during my time in Auvers.'

'Towards the end of my visit to Auvers, I took one last walk up to the plateau, to the graveyard. Your grave and that of your brother Theo look very different from the others: they are covered in ivy. People come from all over the world to visit these two graves over on the east wall of the cemetery. It was a very moving experience.'

'Famous in death but not in life,' sighed Vincent. 'It pleases me very much that my paintings are much loved after my death.' He looked at me with sad eyes.

'Vincent, they are ... oh, they are. Your work is loved by millions of people all over the world, well that world anyway. For all I know, this is the case here, wherever here is.' Vincent smiled and looked ahead again, towards the valley below where we were still sitting, side by side in the evening light.

'If it were not for your sister-in-law, the world might never have had the benefit of your paintings coming to light after your death. By the way, did you know that hundreds of your letters have been been published, along with sketches and prints, as a set of wonderful books. I treated myself to the set a while ago and started to work my way through your letters. They make for very interesting reading. You wrote lots of letters.'

'Now why would anyone be interested in reading my letters?'

'You would be surprised. Academics take an interest. And lovers of your work, such as me. I found them fascinating.

'You know, this thing about your success as an artist. It seems to me that it is as if you knew all along that it would happen eventually ... you seemed to know all along. It is a tragedy that you were poor - was it only one painting that you sold, or your brother sold on your behalf? You might have been poor in life, but you left a wonderful legacy for the world to treasure and admire, largely due to the efforts of your sister-in-law Jo. She made sure that the world did not forget the genius that was Vincent van Gogh.'

Vincent awarded himself a knowing smile. We sat together in the quickening dusk, the great painter and an admirer. There was no need for conversation; it was enough that I have met one of my heroes and watched him at work. We watched the dusk deepen until we saw the lights of distant farms and cottages in the valley below.

Chapter Five

Annelies Marie

The path to the residence of the Frank family is lined with scented shrubs unknown to my untutored senses. To walk along the finely-gravelled path from the front gate released bursts of fragrance as I brushed past soft bushes that adorn the narrow path, filling my head with aromas that served to quell my excitement and anxiety about visiting this celebrated family.

Kal had contacted Otto Frank at my request. I had expected a polite refusal but was surprised and thrilled to receive an invitation. I so very much wanted to meet Anne Frank and her family, even if the unlikely prospect of a teenage girl agreeing to meet a middle-aged man only resulted in a polite exchange of niceties. As it turned out, Anne was charming and rather wonderful.

I thought about the imminence of meeting Anne as I reached the front door of the Frank's house and told myself that I will not be disappointed if she is out with her young friends so that she wouldn't have to exchange small talk with a strange man that she had never heard of.

I hesitated before pulling on the bell rope and stepped back to take in the setting. The three-storey, red brick house is surrounded by richly-coloured borders to the front and on either side, leaving it to me to imagine that someone in the household has continued their gardening expertise at the rear of the house. The path that I have just walked along opens out to reveal a wide gravel area that stretches along the full width of the house and continues around each side.

I stepped forward on to the threshold again and gave the bell rope a gentle tug, almost as if I didn't want to disturb the occupants who might be within. I can easily retrace my steps, I thought to myself, as I felt my heart beat a little faster at the prospect of ... the door opened almost, it seemed, the moment I let go of the rope. Time appeared to slow down as I recognised the figure holding the door wide open: the shock of slightly unruly black hair, the deep, dark eyes and dazzling, uninhibited smile. 'Please come in,' said Anne Frank with a hand gesture. 'We are expecting you.'

I was, momentarily, rooted to the spot, unable to overcome an apparent paralysis of my limbs. There was a lump in my throat and I knew that any attempt to speak would be choked with tears. Anne leant forward, took my right hand in hers and gently pulled me through the front door. 'Please come in,' she said again.

I recovered my composure with sufficient control and managed a brief and faint 'Thank you.'

'This way,' said Anne, letting go of my hand. 'We're out in the garden.'

I followed Anne across a deep hall that spanned the width of the house towards a lightly-panelled passage that opened opposite the front door and led past a number of doors to the right and left. Anne walked lightly on bare feet, a pale summer dress outlining her slim figure. She cast a single glance over her right shoulder and smiled reassuringly as if to make sure that I was still following her as instructed. I already felt that I was just a little bit in love with Anne Frank, one of the most famous young women in my former world and someone who lives long in the hearts of the millions of people who have read her diary.

'Margot and Mother are in there,' said Anne as we passed a kitchen. The passage ended at an open glass door that lead to the garden at the rear of the house where a group of people were sitting on cane chairs arranged on a large patio. The talk and laughter died down as we approached the group.

'This is father,' said Anne as Otto Frank got up from his chair. 'You are very welcome James,' he said, smiling broadly. 'Kal has told us all about you.'

'Ah, Kal. Is he your guardian too? He seems to be a VIP around here?'

'He's not actually *our* guardian, but he has been very helpful and protective towards us ... please have a seat.' Otto Frank gestured towards an empty chair. 'Refreshments are on their way.'

Anne sat next to her father: some of the other members of the group had gone indoors. 'Ah, Margot's homemade lemonade,' said Otto.

Anne's elder sister and their mother emerged from the house bearing trays of glasses, a tinkling jug of iced lemonade and a cake and plates. A large glass of lemonade and a slice of sponge cake was placed wordlessly on a marble-topped table next to my chair. Margot smiled warmly as she set down my refreshments. Margot was as recognisable as Anne from the many photographs that I have seen of her.

The group that was seated in the garden in the warm afternoon sunshine now comprised the four members of the Frank family, an elderly, white-haired woman and me. No-one spoke for what seemed like several minutes while lemonade was sipped and cake was broken with silver forks and savoured politely. Here I was, immersed in a bucolic scene of such apparent ordinariness that reminded me of lazy summer holidays spent with my cousins in my uncle and aunt's garden in the south of Scotland many years ago. But it wasn't my uncle and aunt who were taking tea with me in their garden, it was the Frank family and Miep Gies who sat before me. I hardly knew what to say to express how I felt to be in the presence of some of the occupants of the secret annexe to Otto Frank's offices in Amsterdam and their principal helper, Miep, who looked after them during the latter stages of the second world war and kept them hidden from the Nazis until they were betrayed and sent to concentration camps.

'It is wonderful to see you all together, to see you together as a family and with Miep too.' I broke the silence. 'I can't begin to express how it feels to see you together.' I felt a catch in my throat as I said these things. 'Lovely cake, I heard myself say with spectacular banality, 'lovely lemony flavour.'

'We have lemon trees,' said Margot, pointing towards the end of the long back garden of the house, 'at the far end of the lawn.'

A soft, warm breeze rustled the shrubs and trees that surround the lawn that lay beyond the patio. 'You have a wonderful garden, it surrounds the whole house.'

'Anne is the expert,' said Edith, their mother. 'She gets some of her ideas from George.'

'He's a wonderful gardener,' I said. 'I've wandered around George's garden lots of times ... met some interesting people too. Kal arranged my first visit; he always seems to know how to arrange these things.

'Talking of trees, I have some bad news to impart to all of you. The old chestnut tree behind the annexe to your hiding place in Amsterdam blew down in a gale in the August of 2010. I'm so sorry to tell you this, because I know how much glimpses of this tree meant to you. Anne, you mentioned the tree many times in your diary. The sight of the old tree must have seemed like a tiny window on to the free world outside. There have been problems with the upkeep of the tree for decades, but the gale brought the matter to a close. It's gone now. It's a sad thing.'

Everyone looked upset as I imparted this news. I immediately wished that I hadn't mentioned it.

'It had to happen eventually,' said Otto. 'It was a very old tree. It must have lasted over sixty years after we left.'

I saw that Anne and Margot were both wiping tears away from their cheeks. 'I wish I hadn't told you,' I said meekly. 'I should have known that it would upset you. I am so very sorry; I should leave now.'

'No, James, please don't go ... it isn't your fault. We would have been informed in time; someone would have let us know. Our guardian probably knew, but he has kept it from us, don't you think so Pim?' Anne looked at Otto.

'Perhaps so, Anne,' said Otto, stroking her hand while addressing me: 'Kal is the go-between between ourselves and the community. Not many people know who we are and where we are. The delivery men know us by a false family name and they don't seem to recognise us.'

'I didn't expect to receive an invitation. I feel extremely honoured and privileged to be given the opportunity to meet you all. I have so much to ask you about, you know, your hiding place, but I can resist that.' I glanced around the group. 'I only asked Kal in the expectation of not succeeding ... I am so very grateful.'

'We have friends and family who visit us, but anyone else is an exception. You are now one of our exceptions and you may visit us any time you like. Isn't that right Pim,' said Anne, using her father's nickname again.

'Of course, Anne. James here admires your writing, so that is another good reason for welcoming him.'

'I asked Kal who wrote the letters to the local newspaper praising my articles ... and here you are,' said Anne.

'I didn't know they were yours at first, then I put two and two together. Your pseudonym of "Kitty" is a bit of a giveaway. You write wonderfully well, everyone in the world, the other world, knows that. You said somewhere in your diary that you would like to be a writer after the war. Little did you know that this happened even if ... even though, you know, you weren't there to find out.'

'How could my simple diary have become so well-known? I hear that there are films and plays and all sorts.'

'There have been a number of films and plays, some more successful than others. The best thing, in my opinion, is to read the diary. Reading it is the best thing,' I said. 'Margot, I read somewhere that you kept a diary but it was lost when you left your hiding place?'

'I did keep a diary. I don't know how it came to be lost. Anne has more than made up for its loss.' Margot smiled at Anne.

'It would have been great to have been able to read both diaries though, get another perspective on things,' I said, feeling glad that I have brought Margot into the conversation. 'Anyway, it seems that Anne is fulfilling her dream of becoming a writer after all.'

'I do lots of other things as well,' said Anne, 'but I love writing.'

'I have recently joined a writing group. I imagine that if you joined, it would be rather overwhelming for us,' I said.

'I am sure that I would be overwhelmed by you all,' said Anne.

'No ... no, not you - *we* would be in awe of *you*. I certainly am.' I felt myself redden as I said this.

'You are very kind James.'

Polite conversation reverberated around the group of people who were seated on the patio. For reasons which are not entirely clear to me, the Frank family treated me like some long lost relative. The only member of our afternoon tea party who hadn't said a great deal was the white-haired, elderly woman, another hero of mine, Miep Gies.

'Why, I am forgetting myself James,' said Otto. 'I haven't properly introduced everyone. These are my daughters, Anne and Margot, of course you know them by name. My wife, Edith, and may I introduce Miep.'

'Hello,' said the elderly woman. 'My English is very bad.'

I got up from my chair and went over to where Miep was seated and grasped her tiny outstretched hand in mine. 'Miep, this is indeed an honour. I know you from photographs in your book. I know that you have said and written that you are not a hero, but you are you know. Your selfless actions in protecting the annexe and its occupants are widely-known.'

'I didn't know that, I only did what anyone would.'

I finally let go of Miep's hand, having overextended the enthusiasm of my greeting and returned to my chair. 'The Netherlands' first family, including Miep,' I ventured.

'After the Royal Family,' rejoined Margot, as she refilled my glass with lemonade.

'That's agreed then,' I suggested.

I was relieved that Margot has refilled my glass. My mouth was dry from the utter emotion of being in the presence of the principal characters in a real-life drama that played out in the city of Amsterdam towards the end of the second world war. The clinking of ice splashing into my glass brought my mind back from my visits to number 263 Prinsengracht, where the Frank family and friends hid from the occupying Nazis, to the bucolic scene in which I found myself. 'Thank you Margot, your lemonade is very thirst-quenching.'

'You are our first outside visitor who hasn't asked us about ... about the end of the war,' said Otto Frank. 'People ask question after question.'

'I wouldn't dream of it,' I said. 'As I've said already, I feel enormously grateful to actually meet and talk with you all; that is enough for me. I don't want to bother you with the past.'

'It's always there,' said Edith Frank, 'but look at us now. We're together as a family, happy and safe. There is no need to dwell upon such horrors that befell us after we were taken away from Amsterdam.'

'Exactly,' I said. 'The people that I've met in our little community are leading much better lives now than ... well ... than before. Besides, fame and celebrity don't seem to matter here.'

'They don't, do they?', suggested Anne. 'I've met George lots of times, and his friend John. I understand that they were famous the world over before; here, no-one bothers them.'

'Famous! I'll say. John, George and two others - Ringo and Paul - used to be the most famous popular musicians in the world.'

As the afternoon wore on, we shared our experiences of our community and of the people that we have met in our new lives. I told them about the evening that Charles Dickens came to the creative writing group. Otto replied by telling me that he has heard Dickens perform some of his public readings and reminded me that he used to read Dickens whilst in hiding in Amsterdam.

Eventually, I judged that it was time for me to leave. 'May I thank you all very much for having me this afternoon; it has been wonderful to meet all of you. I won't tell anyone that I have been here, but I'll tell myself from time to time.'

This made everyone laugh. 'You are a funny man, Mr. James,' says Miep. 'Come again and make me laugh.'

'You know that you can come here at any time,' said Edith.

'Thank you,' I replied as I folded my napkin, placed it on the table next to me and got up to leave.

'I'll show you out,' said Anne.

We retraced our steps along the passage and returned to the hall at the front of the house. I noticed the two van Gogh paintings on the way in but I stopped to have a proper look at them where they occupied a space amongst framed photographs and a large mirror. 'Vincent's,' I said, 'one of you and one of Margot. He always wanted to paint more portraits during his short life, but he couldn't afford models to sit for him. These two portraits are wonderful.'

'We love them too,' said Anne. 'Vincent is a very generous man. He has given us several paintings. We have put only two in the hall. Others are elsewhere in the house.'

Anne opened the front door to let me out. As I stood below the front step, I turned to look at Anne who was framed in the doorway. She seemed taller now, by dint of the step and almost faced me eye-to-eye.

'Miss. Frank, may I ... ?'

'Oh *please* call me Anne.'

'Very well. Anne, may I ask a favour?'

'Of course, what is it?'

'Kal asked me when I arrived in the community to write down my experiences and feelings, my reflections and so on. To begin with, I kept a diary. However, as time went on, I abandoned the diary and re-wrote everything along the lines of a memoir, a proper account of my time here. I joined a creative writing group to help me with my writing ... I've never done anything like this before ... but I've kept the memoir up to date ever since I scrapped the diary. Well, not quite scrapped the diary. I still keep a diary to help me to write my memoir, if you see what I mean. Can I show you my account of today? Would you read it ... will you be my sternest critic?'

'I'm flattered that you ask. I will do my best. I am going to George's garden on Sunday afternoon. Can you bring your writing then? I often like to sit in the summerhouse by the lake. Do you know it?'

'I do know it. I've seen you there, from a distance. I didn't know that it was you, of course, but I did see you a few weeks ago. Were you working?'

'I usually go there to write. It can be busy and noisy in the house. I love the house, of course, but I prefer to be on my own to write. No-one bothers me in George's garden. Vincent and I chat from time to time and George usually brings me a drink if he sees me while he is working in his garden, but apart from that it is very peaceful and a lovely place to write.

'By the way, I have seen some of your writing. Cynthia gave me something that you had written about a man called Nelson Mandela. You mention me in it. I did so like that piece of writing.'

'Well, thank you. Coming from you, that is praise indeed. That explains what Cynthia was up to. She asked me for a copy "to show to someone". All very mysterious, until now. Will three o'clock be alright?'

'Until three o'clock on Sunday then. James, can I just say that I am so glad that you didn't ask me or any of the others about the concentration camps ... it was so horrible. I would like to talk to you about it one day though, but not yet.'

An image flashed through my mind of Anne and Margot: their heads are shaved and rags hang from their thin bodies. Both girls are cold and hungry and are dying of typhus. I can hardly bear to think of them both in such condition in Auschwitz and Belsen concentration camps.

'I've recently read a book - not here but before I came here - about two sisters who survived Auschwitz: Rena and Danka Kernreich. The book paints a day-to-picture of life in the camp, so I have some idea of what it was like for you and your family. I wish that you and your sister and your mother could have survived, just as Rena and Danka did.'

'But we did survive James, my family are here together; we are happy ... we *did* survive.' Anne gripped me by the hand. 'We are here ... that is enough for us.'

'We will only talk about it when you are ready Anne, one day perhaps. Please don't feel that you have to talk about the camps for my benefit. I have enough of a picture of what your existence must have been like: what I know hurts as it is, to know more might be too much for me to bear.'

'Let's not think about it then James.' Anne gripped my other hand and gazed directly into my moist eyes. 'You mustn't upset yourself by thinking about such horrors. I am so glad that we have met. I now have a new friend.' Anne let go of my hands and her serious face broke into a smile.

'Yes, we don't ever have to talk about it Anne. Let's dwell on the here and now.

'I'd be glad for your thoughts on my writing efforts. By the way, you all speak such good English. I hope that you don't think that I'm being patronising.'

'Not at all, thank you. Until Sunday then.' Anne Frank leant forward, held my upper arms and kissed me lightly on both cheeks and was gone. I faced the closed front door of the

Frank family house, then turned and walked back along the narrow path to the gate that leads to the lane, unable to stem the tears that washed away the brief touch of those lips.

※

As I neared the shore of the lake opposite the summerhouse I saw Anne, sitting at a table bent over whatever she was doing. Just at the moment I reached the shore, she looked up and waved. I made my way along the path along the edge of the lake until I reached where she was sitting. The summerhouse was open on the side facing the lake and contained a hexagonal table and matching chairs made of some kind of white wood. I sat down, half-facing Anne; she had come equipped with pens and notebooks spread out before her.

'I often come here to write ... oh, I told you that when you came to the house,' said Anne is response to my unasked question. 'It's quieter than the house and George says that I can treat this summerhouse as my own. He is a kind and gentle man, in tune with nature. Look how harmonious grows his garden. It is so rich with colour and scent.'

'It is obvious from your diary that you love nature: and from your short stories. I don't know what anything in the garden is called; I'm hopeless with flowers and plants.'

'I can name them all; I'll teach you one day. You've read some of my short stories?'

'Yes. They are published in a little book called *Tales from the Secret Annexe*. I assume that this material was rescued by Miep along with the diaries?'

'They must have been. I had almost forgotten about them. The jottings of an immature girl, mostly.'

'I loved them. They are an interesting contrast to the diaries. You could be free to write some fiction rather than documenting the reality of everyday life in hiding in the annexe.'

'You are right. The stories gave me a sense of freedom from the confines of our hiding place. As you know, we were living in very close proximity and could easily get on one another's nerves. I could escape when I was writing either my diary or my stories.'

'Anne, I don't agree that your journal of stories and essays, the one that is separate from your diary, is immature. On the contrary, although you were - what? - about fourteen or fifteen at the time, some of the essays towards the end of the book show that you were thinking and writing about huge subjects such as world peace, the way that mankind treats his fellow beings, and the like. These are very serious topics for one so young to tackle. This is why I mentioned you in my written piece about Nelson Mandela. The thing that you both have in common is that you thought the best of mankind, despite everything that happened to both of you.'

Anne smiled and looked at me intently. 'Thank you for including me with Mister Mandela. I feel honoured to be mentioned in such august company.'

'Did you know that your diary sustained him and some of his fellow prisoners during their long years of captivity?'

'I didn't know that. How lovely to think that my daily jottings meant so much to so many people. I always intended my diary to be useful after the war. That is partly why I wrote it. Little did I know what would happen in the course of time, although I wasn't there to experience it.'

'I remember that you wrote somewhere that you wanted to be a writer. Well, it turns out that you became one of the most famous writers in the world.'

Anne sat back in her chair and clasped her hands behind her head. 'Did you bring your writing?'

I handed Anne my notebook. 'I hope that you can read my handwriting. It's only a first draft. I usually write a first draft by hand then try to improve on it when I copy it out. Can I leave you to it? I'll only be embarrassed if I stay.'

Anne tucked her legs under herself and opened my notebook. 'Your writing is fine: I can read it easily. See you later.'

I spent what I judged to be sufficient time for Anne to read my work wandering aimlessly along paths that separate borders of flower and shrubs. I knew my way around George's garden, so I chose a route that would bring me back to the lakeside summerhouse. Anne had evidently finished reading my work; my exercise book was closed and she was busily writing in a thick notebook. Anne looked up as I sat down.

'James, you write very well. I see that you gave it the title *Annelies Marie*. I haven't been called that for a long time.'

'Its a lovely name. I assume that it was shortened to Anne when you were very young.'

'The account of your visit to our house is very touching. Did you really mean the bit about being a little bit in love with me?'

I felt the redness rush to my cheeks: I had forgotten to leave this out in my rashness to ask Anne to read my work. 'Ah, perhaps I should have left that bit out. I didn't mean that you read that bit.'

'No James ... your should always write with honesty and with what is in your heart. I said some hurtful things about my mother in my diary ... it was what I felt at the time. You are only being honest ... there's nothing wrong with being honest is there?'

'What if your father finds out? It's not the kind of love ... you know ... between a man and a woman of similar age. It's more an intense feeling of admiration between friends. It's just that you happen to be a young woman and I happen to be a lot older than you.'

'Father won't find out; I won't tell him and he's not likely to read your journal is he? Anyway, I like what you said.'

'I hope that you are not embarrassed that I left it in. It was difficult to hide the emotion of seeing you when you opened your front door. I've read your diary and seem to know so much about you, Miep and the others that I felt that I already knew you when I saw you standing in your doorway.'

'I don't mind you saying it. We all like and trust you. I trust you. Let's be friends and fellow scribblers. Anyway, I like your account of your visit to our house last week. You are better at dialogue than me.'

'I can't get the descriptive element right yet. To begin with, our group's tutor said that my dialogue was good but she and some of the members of the group said that they couldn't "see" where the dialogue was taking place, they couldn't visualise the context. Since then, I've tried to work on the descriptive element and write what is in my mind's eye.'

'That's *exactly* what I do,' said Anne in an excited tone of voice. 'I think of the scene in my head, as if I am watching a film, then I try to write what the scene looks like and what the characters in it are saying. I think that you should try to avoid overdoing it though. What I mean is that you don't have to describe *everything* in a scene. Sometimes you might paint an outline of a scene or a situation and let the reader fill in of the details for themselves. I don't think that you need to tell the reader everything about everything.'

'Right ... I see what you mean. I work with scenes too. I try to visualise each scene in turn and write what I see. We seem to agree on this as a technique.'

'Then you can add things to your scene,' suggested Anne.

'You mean things such as sound ... the sound of the wind for example, and you could explain whether it is warm of cold and so forth ... fill in what the reader can't see.'

'Exactly, James. Our readers should be able to see, hear and *feel* ... we should help them to use *all* of their senses and feel emotions that our characters are feeling. The words that we write fall on our readers' eyes: this is the only way that we can reach their hearts.'

'I wish that I could do that Anne. You can. You did it in your diary; you touched everyone's heart. You certainly touched mine.'

'The musing of a very young teenage girl.'

'These were not mere musings Anne. The reader is gripped by the extreme circumstances recorded in your account. Millions of people have read your diary. It has been translated into goodness knows how many languages. I remember the first time that I visited 263 Prinsengracht. The building is a museum and book shop. The visitor can climb the stairs behind the secret bookcase and wander around the annex. I found the whole experience intensely moving. I was in tears at the end of the visit.'

'You are a very sensitive and emotional man James. You feel things very deeply. I'm sure that this will help with your journal. You must do what Kal says: "write it down ... it might come in useful".'

'Useful for what? First Kal, now you.'

'You will see James, you will see. All in good time.'

'You sound as secretive as Kal. I wonder what you can both mean.'

'My lips are sealed James so I can't kiss you on the cheek. Anyway, you might cry again.'

'Oh dear, my honesty is too apparent and has got the better of me again,' I replied. I felt my neck prickle with embarrassment and my face redden in tandem. 'You don't want to see a grown man cry again, now do you?'

Anne leant across the table, kissed me on both cheeks and retreated to gather up her writing materials. 'I hope that no-one saw that,' she said with mischief in her eyes. 'Here's your notebook. Your work shows promise James. I was very touched reading your account of our first meeting.'

Anne grabbed my hand and pulled me to my feet. 'Come on, let's go and see if we can find George.'

Chapter Six

Hail to the Chief

The day of my longest bike ride so far dawns sunny and warm. I had taken up bike riding shortly after my arrival; I'd been an avid cyclist in my former life and was eager to stay in shape in my new one. Kal, of course, helped with the acquisition of a classy bike, clothing and accessories from the only bike shop in Morlham.

On the day of the ride, I felt pleased with my fitness as I slot two full drinks bottles into their cages on the frame of my bike. My legs are strong and I feel ready for a few hours in the saddle. I carry out a final check on my gear: drinks sachets, energy bars, bananas and smartphone in the back pockets of my top; emergency pump clipped to the frame behind one of the drinks cages; toolkit and spare inner tubes in the zip-up bag that is attached beneath the saddle; gloves; sweat bands; helmet and shades. Today, I am going to meet another of my earthly heroes: I am ready for the off and ready to forget the recurring dream that I had again last night.

I wave at acquaintances who are strolling around the village as I ride slowly across the village green towards the railway station. I pause and think of Jim and Marilyn: they had met me on this spot on my first day. Since that day, I have met many wonderful people and made new friends. I feel a tremendous surge of well-being and joy begin in my stomach and spread upwards until I feel tears sting my eyes. I am forced to remove and clean my shades and wipe away my joyful tears. With shades back in place and helmet strapped in place beneath my chin, I throw my bike into a right turn and speed towards the border gate of our village.

I slow down a little and wave casually to Harry, who is on duty at the gate, and yell 'I'm off to the coast, back later this afternoon.' This elicits 'Have a good ride' from Harry as he retreats behind me. It is good practice to let the gateman know where you are going, especially if you are entering the desert zone: that is all that is required of a resident. Kal also knows about my plans for the day.

The low hills that flank our dale soon give way to a flat terrain where nothing much grows. After a few miles, this scrubland becomes sand of a purity and intensity of colour that I always marvel at when I venture into the desert strip that lies between our dale and the coast. It was into the desert zone that Jim had brought me, on the back of his motorbike, on the evening of my arrival a few months ago. We were moving at high speed on that occasion so that I was hardly able to take in the scenery as Jim gunned his motorbike along the same desert road that I am riding along now, the road that will take me to the coast. Not that the scenery is much to savour, apart from the pink sand that stretches as far as the eye can see on either side of the sheer black strip of flat road that is rolled out straight ahead of me. There are turnings to the left and right here and there, but there is virtually nothing to distinguish the road to the diner from any of the other roads that fly off to the left and right. I recognise the turning though, as I pedal past it.

The desert strip is about fifty miles wide where I cross it from our dale to the coast; it will take me about three hours to reach my destination if I keep my cadence high and constant. The flat, straight road reflects the heat of the sun and amplifies the hot air that rushes past me as I speed along its smooth surface, my narrow-profile racing tyres making a pleasing hissing noise to accompany my regular breathing. If I take lots of drinks and keep up a good average speed, I should feel a sea breeze by midday.

There isn't much traffic on the road to the coast today. A few delivery vans and small trucks pass me in both directions, their occupants holler incomprehensible greetings as they whizz past. A couple of motorbikes roar past me in the direction of the coast, but neither of them is ridden by Jim, otherwise I'm sure that he would have recognised my cycling shorts and top and would have stopped. I see only one other bike rider coming towards me: we exchange a brief wave, as is the manner of the camaraderie amongst cyclists. At least I am not the only bike rider to tackle the coast road in this heat today.

After an hour or so my drinks bottles are soon empty. Fortunately, about half way to the coast, there is a dusty-looking, ramshackle snack bar that is set back from the road. It has a partner, an equally dusty-looking shack on the opposite side of the road: perfect for the journey back later this afternoon, but how or why the proprietors can run two such establishments on such a quiet road is rather baffling.

Despite the relative remoteness and the low volume of passing traffic, both snack bars have attracted a respectable number of vans and trucks of the type that passed me earlier this morning. Since I've been in my new surroundings in my new life, I haven't given much thought how goods are distributed. The small trucks and vans are, presumably, an integral part of the transport and distribution network around here.

The scene resembles one from an American road movie as I carefully negotiate the dusty car park in front of the snack bar to my left to find a suitable place to leave my bike. Weather-beaten men in boots and denims sit up at a counter on high stools and a few other travellers sit at Formica-topped tables that are scattered around the neat and clean room. I turn a few heads and silence the scattered conversation as I clip-clop across the wooden floor in my bike shoes and brightly-coloured cycling gear. I proffer my empty bottles and ask for them to filled with fruit juice. The bartender, a greasy-looking man wearing what used to be a white apron, asks me to wave my smartphone against his payment terminal and wishes me a good ride. I retrace my noisy steps across the floor and push my bike carefully across the car park to reach the road. The space in front of the snack bar is rather gravelly; I don't want to get a puncture out here in the desert.

Another couple of hours brings a change to the landscape. The pink desert gives way to treeless, gently-rolling green hills that lead to the sea. The sun is still high and hot and the dry, dusty atmosphere changes to a clearer, sweeter air that brings the promise of the taste of the sea and a view of it that will soon reveal itself. I remember the sea air and salty taste in the breeze from my boyhood days long ago in another world. Memories of balmy summer holidays in Hastings with my dear mother flood into my mind. I can hear the sound of waves on a pebbly beach and the cries of children dashing into the shallows as they cast anxious backwards glances to the safety of the beach that is marked by several pairs of footwear that await the return of their owners. One of the children is me: a scrawny boy with glasses and arm bands, wishing that I wasn't about to immerse myself in cold water, a feeling that has never left me.

The last few miles of my journey today roll up and down easy slopes until, at last, there it is - the sea: its sound; its air; its evocation of delight and unabashed joy in the discovery of its presence in *this* world. I stop and unclip both feet from their pedals and stand and stare as if I am about to see the sea for the first time in my life.

The final few hundred yards of the road that emerges from the desert leads me through high, yellow sand dunes to a T junction where I have braked to a halt and am standing with my feet on the road either side of my bike. Straight ahead, across the road, is a broad beach that has welcomed the tide. The sea makes its characteristic sucking and dragging sound as it flows to and fro across the shingle. Away to my right, the road hides behind what looks like an endless row of low dunes that are my destination. To my left, I can see the beginnings of a small harbour in a narrow bay, its buildings spread around the bay and up into the hills behind. A sandy-coloured citadel stands on a rocky bluff at the far end of the bay. I promise myself that I will visit the harbour before I go home this afternoon.

The purpose of riding to the coast today is to visit Professor Richard P. Feynman, known as "The Chief" to his many fans. Kal had spoken with Feynman's guardian to arrange my visit. I am rather daunted by the prospect of meeting Feynman: he was a hero of mine in my former life, largely due to his larger-than-life persona, amusing stories and his approach to life in general and to authority in particular. My knowledge of physics isn't particularly deep, so I hope that Feynman won't expect me to be articulate on his specialist subject of theoretical physics. I have read *QED*, Feynman's book on quantum electrodynamics, but I admit to have struggled to understand fully the notation used by him in his approach to the theory of light and matter.

With these thoughts in mind, I re-engage the cleats on my cycling shoes with my pedals and, suitably re-mounted on my bike, I turn right at the T junction and head for the low dunes that sit back from the shore. Kal had told me that there are several beach houses that nestle amongst the dunes built where the ground is firm enough to support a wooden structure and that I should look out for a driveway with a house sign for Far Rockaway at the roadside.

I soon pass drives that lead off the road and between the dunes. Glimpses of brightly-painted, wooden houses, garages and the occasional parked car can be seen and although the houses are widely-spaced apart, I ride slowly so that I can look out for the sign for Feynman's beach residence. When I find it, I dismount at the end of the steep, gravelly drive from where I can see part of what looks like a large, multi-levelled property. A station wagon decorated with the kind of diagram that I had seen in Feynman's book *QED* is parked at the top of the drive. This is the place: it is midday according to my bike computer and the Chief will be expecting me.

I hoist my bike onto my left shoulder to avoid contact with the gravel and make my way up the drive towards the house. My footsteps must be making a loud enough scrunching sound to bring a familiar figure to the wooden railing of the deck that surrounds the house. Professor Richard P. Feynman is leaning on the rail looking down at me struggling up the steep slope with a bike over my shoulder.

'Come on up,' he says and motions to a short flight of steps that led up to the side of the house to the deck. 'You can leave your machine down there.'

I lean my bike on the side of the house, cast a quick look at the examples of Feynman diagrams that are stencilled on the sides of the station wagon, remove my cycling shoes and helmet and clamber up the steps in my stockinged feet.

'I'm sitting out front,' says Feynman as I follow him along the deck to the front of the house. 'Could you use a beer, riding in all this heat?'

'A soft drink or a soda please, if you have such a thing. I don't drink alcohol when I am out for a ride.'

'Sensible man.' Feynman calls to someone in the house; I didn't catch the name. 'Take a seat.'

'This is great,' I say, taking in the view before I sit down on one of the canvas chairs that are arranged around a low table.

'The deck goes round all four sides of the house,' says Feynman. 'Narrow at the sides and back and spacious out front here overlooking the sea. I spend a lot of time out here. I used to have a beach house in California, before I came here.'

'It's great,' I repeat. The ground at the beach side of the house slopes gently down to a low cliff so that the prospect from this part of the deck takes in sand and sea. There is a gentle breeze floating over us. 'What a great spot.'

'I've lived here ever since my arrival in the mid nineteen eighties. How about you?'

'I'm inland, about fifty miles from here, in a lovely village in a kind of vale or dale, I guess you would call it.'

'Fifty miles! That is a hell of a way to cycle.'

'Oh, I'm getting used to it. I'm trying to keep fit. I used to do a lot of cycling when I was ... er ... in the other place.'

'Some of my students cycled around my university campus, but I never did any cycling myself. Fancy gear you've got on.'

'Yeah, its what we bike riders like to wear. Part of the fun, looking good I mean.'

A slim, middle-aged woman brings out a tray of refreshments and places it on the table. Feynman whispers a few almost inaudible words to the woman, who smiles broadly in return. 'This is yours James; no alcohol', she says.

The drink is cold and very refreshing. 'You know my name?'

'Oh yes. I'll leave you two to it,' she says before disappearing into the house.

'The Guardians do their homework,' says Feynman.

'Who are they,' I say, 'or perhaps I ought not to be asking such a question?'

'You have been here for only a few months,' says Feynman.

I nod in reply.

'I've been here for quite a few years; you'll find out more about the Guardians as time goes by. They don't give much away, but they do reveal some of their little secrets from time to time.'

'I wonder how you get to *be* a Guardian? That's another puzzle.' Feynman doesn't answer.

'It's just that I'm having such a wonderful life here. In the few months that I've been here, my former life seems to be fading from memory. Either that or I don't want to think about it. Anyway, now that I've been here for a while, I'm beginning to ask myself questions about my present life.'

'Can I offer you some advice James? Accept your new life for the time being. You are approaching a critical point in your new existence. Kal will advise you when he thinks you are ready. Trust in your Guardian.'

'Thanks for the advice Professor Feynman.'

'Please call me Dick or Richard if you prefer.'

'Okay, thanks for the advice ... er ... Richard. I don't want to question things too much in case I wake up from what turns out to be a wonderful dream and find myself back there. I don't want this life to vanish like dreams do.

'Isn't it difficult for you? You were - and still are - a great scientist. You questioned stuff, you explored and explained the laws of physics. What do *you* make of all this? Sorry, I'm asking fundamental questions again.'

Feynman leans back in his canvas chair and gazes out to sea. He looks tanned, healthy and relaxed in a pale blue shirt and stone-coloured slacks. His long hair is silvery-grey and lustrous: he looks just like he did in photographs in the early nineteen eighties before he became seriously ill with cancer.

Feynman turns to face me with that broad grin that features in many of the photographs and films of him that I have seen. 'I'm still interested in finding things out, but the ultimate question - the answer to everything - still eludes me. I'm less bothered about that than when I used to do physics for a living. There may never have been an ultimate answer or a unified theory of everything. It may be the case that physicists will still have to carry on finding stuff out, okay.

'I'm less concerned about most of that stuff now. I'm still curious; I'll never be cured of that, but I'm not frightened if I don't find out how *this* world works.'

'The laws of physics as you understood them back then, do they apply here?'

'Superficially, they appear to be the same set of fundamental laws of nature. If I were to work on some of the problems that I left behind, that would be all well and good but there would be no experimental results to test my theories. So, it's academic.

'There is something that I can tell you though: we live in a Type One civilisation.'

'What on earth ... hah! ... is that?'

'Oh about fifty years ago, around nineteen sixty two I think, a Russian astronomer came out with some theoretical models and definitions of types of civilisation based upon their control or mastery of energy: the energy required for sustaining human life. The so-called Kardashev scale - he was called Nicolai Kardashev - specifies three types of civilisation: One, Two and Three. Evidently we are living in a Type One civilisation.'

'And where we used to be?'

'Some say Type Zero; others calculated it as between zero and one. In the early seventies Carl Sagan ... you know of him, a great science communicator ... he calculated it to be 0.7. Such calculations are based on the use the Earth's resources to produce energy and so forth. The Earth was less than one and we weren't very good at it ... we weren't very good at being efficient with the energy we produced.'

'Meaning that we wasted a lot of energy?'

'Sure we wasted energy. We wasted lives fighting wars for it - oil I mean - in places like the Middle East. We made mistakes when nuclear power stations blew up - Three Mile Island; Chernobyl - and so forth. A lot of waste and human error.'

'So what is the definition of a Type One civilisation according to Kan ... Kan ... ?'

'Kardashev ...'

'... according to Kardashev's hypothetical civilisations?'

Feynman doesn't seem to mind me asking lots of questions: he seems genuinely interested in explaining things to me. One of the many things that fans of the Chief held dear was Feynman's gift for teaching. At the moment, I am fortunate enough to be in a class of one.

'The principal feature of a Type One civilisation is where the humans occupying a planet have total and complete mastery over the energy resources of that planet, with obvious consequences. There is enough food for all the population; there is enough energy for the industrial and domestic needs of the population; pollution is minimal; the weather systems are controlled where and when necessary; and so on.

'Think about it: where we are now exhibits all the signs of a Type One civilisation put into practice. For us, it's more than a theory; it's here, all around us.

'A Type One makes extensive use of nuclear fusion, rather than nuclear fission which produces waste products that we can't do much with. We tinkered around with fusion when I was back there in the late twentieth century but we didn't get very far. Here, fusion is clean, sustainable and effective.'

'Anything else in the definition that you know is put into practice here?' I ask Feynman.

'Solar energy: we were useless at exploiting the vast energy of the sun in our solar system. Here, the solar energy from *this* planet's sun - that one up there - is extensively converted into useable energy such as electricity by means of solar panel farms. Places such as the desert zone that you came across this morning host acres and acres of solar panels. You probably won't be able to see 'em from the road Wind power is used extensively as well.

'There is no energy crisis here; there is an ample and sustainable supply of energy for all of our needs. We are in harmony with nature in this place.'

'This is great. If only these principles could be applied back there. What about petrol or gasoline as you Americans call it?'

'Transportation is either electrically or magnetically driven or driven by gas of some kind. My station wagon down there runs on a hydrogen cell. A few things run on gasoline: motorbikes, for example. This means that we can control the amount of oil that is burnt for fuel. Perhaps it is kept for motorbikes purely for the fun of it? Your bike runs on muscle power though. There are no plans to change that.'

'You still have Feynman diagrams on your station wagon, just like you used to back then.'

'You recognise 'em?'

'Not what particle interaction they specifically depict, just the fact that they are Feynman diagrams. The only technical book of yours that I've read is *QED*, the one on quantum electrodynamics, in which you introduce the diagrammatic notation. I'm scientifically trained, so I understood most of the book but not all of it ... just mostly.'

Feynman grins and - was he being kind? - makes no comment on my attempt to understand his theory of quantum electrodynamics.

'So the trucks that passed me on the road this morning are hydrogen-powered?'

'Or battery-powered, or a combination. The transportation systems around here are highly efficient.'

'The delivery and service vehicles that buzz around our village and tootle up and down our valley are very quiet; I guess that they are electric, as is the train that brought me here in the first place?' My first impression of the cool-looking and elegantly-dressed Kal flickers into my mind.

'Correct on all counts James,' says Feynman. 'Another drink?'

'Some cold mineral water if you have some please.'

Feynman disappears into the house from where I can hear voices and the chinking of bottles. The temporary absence of the Chief gives me a chance to stretch my legs and have a look around. I have had a long, hot ride and sitting still has made my legs stiff. The few wobbly steps I take to the front rail of the deck overlooking the sea must look rather comical from the house.

'You okay,' says Feynman returning with another tray of refreshments.

'Fine thanks. I've had a long ride and sitting still without warming down can make you a bit stiff. It's a bike rider's thing.'

'Warming down! I've never heard of warming down. Warming up okay, but not down.'

'It makes me sound like an expert bike rider,' I say as I return to my seat and take a large gulp of my cold drink. 'This is good mineral water. I'm not really an expert. I had a friend back there who is a much better bike rider than I will ever be. He is really strong. He's done mountain passes and that kind of thing. I couldn't keep up with him. He'd always ride slower than his usual speed when we were riding together ... just being kind and thoughtful. That's the kind of guy he was ... is. He's not here yet, thank goodness. I do miss him though. He was a great friend, the best of friends.

'Do you think about people that you used to know, or miss them? Oh, sorry ... that's a personal question?'

A serious moment passes as if a shadow is drawn across the deck where we are sitting.

Feynman's mischievous grin soon returns and the phantom shade gives way to the bright sunlight.

'That's okay. Sure I do. Some folks I miss, some I don't. Some live around here, so we see still see each other as we did before, when we worked together in California at the university. We got old together and some of us wound up here more or less at the same time.'

'How do *they*, whoever they are ... how do they decide who gets to be here or not, as the case may be?'

'Not even I know the answer to that one James,' replies Feynman. The Chief was never an immodest man, so what would be the point of him denying his brilliance.

'Glad the water is good. It comes from the hills near your place. Have a banana. I understand that they are good for bike riders: instant energy. One of my students told me. She used to ride a mountain bike to my university.'

'Your student was right. Thanks. I will.'

'It is getting hotter,' announces Feynman. He gets out of his chair and operates a switch on the wall between the double, French windows. An awning eases out from some kind of mechanism above the windows and settles above our heads. 'That's better,' says Feynman returning to his chair.

'Something else that you must have noticed since you came here: things like beer and mineral water come in recycled bottles. There are no aluminium cans whatsoever.' Feynman picks up a cold beer from the table.

'I noticed the thing about recycling bottles almost from my first day. Such a sensible idea.

'So, they've mastered the energy provided by the sun?'

'Pretty much,' replies Feynman, 'and there are elements of a Type Two civilisation at work here as well.'

'Type Two! Before I ask you about that, can I just say - and I apologise for not saying it before - thank you so much for agreeing to see me today. You must be very busy and you don't know me from Adam.'

'That's okay. Kal has told me something about you. You were scientifically trained, so you seem to understand what we are talking about. It's interesting talking about this stuff because it is put into practice in this world.'

'So then, this Type Two stuff?'

'Okay, yeah ... okay. One of the features of a Type Two civilisation is the capture of solar power by satellites. The sun's rays are captured by solar panels that are deployed by each satellite and beamed to receivers on the ground by either microwaves or laser beams.'

'Wow! Sounds like science fiction to me.'

'You're right. There are many examples of science fiction where we used to be that feature similar satellites. The authors may not have been smart enough to know about Kardashev's work but that doesn't matter, they *were* smart enough to envisage such satellites in their fiction.'

'I thought that our apparent Type One civilisation converts the sun's rays by means of solar panel farms.'

'They do, but think about it. A typical solar panel farm takes up a lot of ground, so an otherwise useless area of desert will do. You can lay out your vast area of panels where no-one lives, but then you've got to do what?'

'Transfer the energy in a suitable form for transportation to where it is needed,' I reply, feeling rather pleased with myself.

'Correct, my friend. This is done here, but it is combined with a ring of satellites around the planet. In short, a mixed approach to energy production is able to meet increasing demands for energy.

'It is for this reason we can state that we live in a place that exhibits strong elements of a Type Two civilisation. We are probably something of the order of a Type One point five, in my view. Freeman Dyson, a former contemporary of mine, published some work about Type Two and energy-producing satellites. Needless to say, we never got round to doing anything about it back then: way too expensive, in Earthly terms.'

'Freeman Dyson: he features in some of the books and films about you that I have, or had I mean. Like you, he was a famous physicist.'

'A brilliant man. What films?'

'TV films mostly, for the BBC, made by Christopher Sykes. One of them featured Ralph Leighton.'

'For the BBC. I remember doing those with Christopher; it was interesting. Ralph: he was a great friend. I wonder what he is doing right now.'

'When I left, he was carrying on your name. He recorded your stories. That's how I got interested in you. I first read them, then I listened to you telling them to Ralph when he recorded them.

'You have a large following, a fan base you know. People love your stories and admire your attitude to authority, as well as your academic work as a theoretical physicist of course.

'What do you do with your time here? Sorry ... I'm getting personal again.'

'That's okay. The authorities consult me and the others from time to time. There are scientists, engineers and so forth here so it makes sense for them to be consulted to solve problems. Sometimes I am contacted as an expert individual, other times we work as a group.'

'So *that's* how this place works. The authorities - whoever they are - use the knowledge and expertise of the engineers and scientists who are here; why wouldn't they? Evidently there are unlimited financial resources to fund our society here. Someone must have the knowledge to create and fund a "Type greater than One" civilisation without making the mistakes of the one we have left behind us. I haven't thought too much about this until now. I *have* thought about it a bit but I've been rather afraid to probe too deeply. I've just kind of accepted what has happened to me since I arrived. You probably think that I don't have an enquiring mind.'

'Sure you have. You're taking your time, assessing things and seeing how things go, meeting interesting people. I hope I'm included.'

'You! Have you any idea? It's such a great thrill to meet you. As I've already said, I've listened to your stories as told to Ralph Leighton and I've watched the set of BBC films where you talk mainly about science. I know, or used to know that is, several people who would be tremendously jealous of me sitting here right now. Many of my university colleagues admired your enthusiasm for physics, your attitude to authority and your verve for life - and your drumming, of course.

'Then there was the whole Tannu Tuva thing, the search for that mysterious country in the middle of Asia. You didn't get to go, but Ralph did. He organised a plaque to be put up somewhere. I can't remember exactly where; somewhere in the capital city I seem to remember. It's made of a dark stone and is pyramid-shaped. It has your name, dates and your face carved into its face.'

'Thanks Ralph,' says Feynman.

'The sad thing is though, I read some reports that the plaque went missing shortly after Ralph returned from Tannu Tuva.'

'Never mind. His heart was in the right place. He couldn't be responsible for its upkeep.'

'The whole "let's go to Tannu Tuva" seemed to me to typify your inquisitive mind. What a pity it took so long for Ralph to get permission to go so that you missed the trip. You were here by then.

'Anyway, I can see why you and your former colleagues have a role to play here, so I can understand why you are here. Why me though, what am I doing here?'

'What did you used to do?' asks Feynman.

'Software engineer. Firstly a practitioner in industry and then a university lecturer.'

'Well then, you've answered your own question.'

'But I haven't been asked to do any work. It's been leisure ever since I arrived.'

'Too soon. The way that work is organised around here is that work is for the common good, leaving time for the arts and other stuff. This is your assessment period.'

'Right, I see. Kal has implied this on more than one occasion. Do you actually consider that you have a job as such, given that you are consulted by the authorities here? I seem to remember your scepticism of the government of the United States of America ... you didn't want to get involved with Washington.'

'Not a full-time job. I do what I can when asked. There is no need to resist; it is for the greater good and the collective good. I have plenty of time for leisure activities.'

'Professor Feynman ... Richard ... let's not beat around the bush. This place is clearly populated by ... let't not put too fine a point on it ... populated by *dead* people, some of whom are ... were ... famous, like you were.'

'Even so-called famous people die. How did you die?'

'I know how and when you died Richard. As for me, I remember being taken ill when I returned to the UK from a business trip to

Africa. The memory of it is hazy and getting hazier as time has gone on here. They don't control our minds do they? Sorry ... that was a silly remark. Anyway, I vaguely recall being put into an ambulance and that is pretty much it, I can't remember anything more about it. The next thing I remember is being met by Kal and taken to a place to live. Since then, I've been trying to come to terms with my new life, meeting people I admired in my former life - such as Professor Richard P. Feynman - and I've kept a journal. Kal advised me on that score. By the way, do you mind if I write about today when I get home?'

'Not at all, go ahead. I hope this will be the first of many conversations.'

I help myself to more water and another banana. 'This is a great house. Do you do much painting out here? You starting painting towards the end of your old life, I was just wondering if you paint in your new life.'

'How come you've seen my paintings?'

'Your daughter, Michelle, put together a book of some of your drawings and paintings. It was great to add your art to your physics and your stories. It's a lovely book. I wish you could see it. It's mostly portraits. Do you do any landscapes or seascapes?'

'Funny you ask. I only do seascapes and a few portraits of friends these days. I'm not ready to show you any seascapes yet; they're a bit rough.'

'Richard, I just happen to know a brilliant painter. Perhaps I could bring him with me next time. You could discuss painting with him. He has done portraits as well as landscapes. I won't say his name in case he isn't keen on travelling out here to the coast or in case he wishes to remain private. Would you like me to see if I can arrange it?'

'Sure. That would be interesting.'

'This is a great deck as well as a great house. It's obvious that they know what we like when it comes to houses. You used to have a beach house in California I seem to remember.'

'Yeah. It wasn't as good as this one though. That's all one room through there.' Feynman points towards the double French windows. 'As you can see, the deck stretches the whole width of the house. Bedrooms are above and there are garages and my studio down below. It's where I paint when I'm not painting out in the open.'

'I live in a cottage in what could be described as a clone of a typical Yorkshire Dales village. Yorkshire is in the northern part of England. You obviously love your beach house.'

'It's great. The sound and smell of the sea ... I can work and think here. It reminds me of beaches in California.'

'My home reminds me of Yorkshire. I didn't live there. My family used to take holidays there when I was a boy.

'Richard there are so many more questions that I would like to ask you, but I think that I should be going now. I've got fifty miles to do to get home. It has been great to meet you; an honour and a privilege in fact.'

Feynman stands up and puts out his hand. His handshake is firm and his smile broadens. 'You take care now. We will meet again. Are you sufficiently refreshed?'

'Yeah, I'm fine thanks.' I gather my helmet and shoes from where I left them under the table and make my way down the steps to where I left my bike. I turn and raise a hand to Feynman who is standing at the top of the steps. He raises a hand in return, turns and disappears around the corner of the house. *Hail to the Chief*, I say to myself, as I shoulder my bike and tread carefully down the drive towards the road. There is no suppressing a feeling of elation and excitement that remains with me for the remainder of the day and that persists even as I write my journal that same evening.

❋

I ride the short distance along the road that runs behind the row of beach houses towards the harbour and instead of taking the desert road towards our dale, I continue straight ahead towards the quay. The harbour road ends at a row of low, stone pillars, indicating that this part of the quay is a pedestrian zone. I dismount my bike obediently and push it along the busy quay, passing several bars and restaurants, crowded with lunchtime custom. I find an empty outside table at a bar that is squashed between two smart restaurants and order a sandwich and a fruit juice.

My table looks directly onto the quay. There is a row of flower tubs that separate the outside tables of each restaurant and bar from a wide pedestrian walkway that runs along the water's edge where a myriad of vessels are moored to mushroom-shape bollards. I chose a table as near to the water's edge as possible; this gives me an uninterrupted view of the quay and somewhere to lean my bike so that it is not in anyone's way.

Several boat owners busy themselves with the mysterious tasks that yacht owners seem to be perpetually preoccupied with. Others appear to be far more sensible in that they are sitting on deck and relaxing in the early afternoon sun. Perhaps the tasks that the busy boat people are engaged in must be accomplished before the relaxation stage can be reached? In any event, I prefer to be firmly on dry land and have always had a fear of being at sea. Even short ferry crossings proved to be a source of anxiety in my former life and as for swimming: "Swimming is staying alive in the water" my grandfather used to say, not exactly words of encouragement to his grandson but sufficient to keep me from being actually unnecessarily immersed in water. It's bad enough being expected to float on the surface of water in various kinds of boat, but being made to get *into* water for fun is a step to far. None of my water-related anxieties trouble me now as I sit watching people strolling along the quay or busying themselves on deck to the accompaniment of stays clinking on a forest of masts.

I pay my bill with my smartphone and ask the waiter to top up my drinks bottles with ice-cold water for the return ride across the desert. As I ride swiftly along in the heat of the afternoon sun, I find that I don't have to think much about the journey back. There will be no turnings to make until I get near to our village and there are precious few inclines to tax my limited climbing ability. Vehicles that overtake me do so with plenty of elbow room, unlike in my former life: road users are respectful of bike riders here. With my mind free to wander as I keep up a respectable speed on the largely straight road, I reflect on my meeting with the Chief.

Professor Richard Feynman was famously rather suspicious of authority and of government in particular, yet he seemed to be involved in the organisation or 'governing' of our new lives here. After all, this place, this planet, this wherever we are has all the trappings of a technologically-advanced, civil society, a Type One point something apparently. Some kind of organisation or structure *must* be managing our society here; clearly, such a body cannot do this without the relevant expertise. Although Feynman was understandably rather evasive when I asked him about his involvement in the government of this place, I came to the conclusion that he and some of his former colleagues are probably part of the network of scientists, engineers and other experts who are called upon to advise those who - for want of a better word - govern (this new life of ours).

Despite Feynman's former scepticism of authority, I didn't want to press him on the matter of his involvement in how things work here; this would have been churlish. Instead, I feel immensely glad that I have met the Chief and was given the opportunity to explore some of the mysteries of my new life and my new surroundings. I wonder to myself if Kal will be any more forthcoming about such matters from now on.

Chapter Seven

John and George

Early one morning, during one of my regular walks in George's garden, he calls to me from where he is working at the edge of the smaller of the two lakes.

'I'm just about to go to the house. There's someone there that I'd like you to meet. He wants to ask you a few things, so will you come now?'

George leads the way. I'd seen what I assumed to be George's house a few times during walks in his garden. A glimpse of distant roofs through tall trees on one occasion; a view of a large fountain and the front of the house at the end of a wide, grassy drive on another. Although George has been kind enough to give me unlimited access to his garden I always kept well away from his house, unwilling to disturb his privacy.

We soon came to the beginning of the grassy drive that I had stumbled upon on a previous visit. The drive slopes down then upwards towards the front of the house in such a way that the dip in the ground appears to foreshorten the distance to the house. The approach to the house presents itself in almost perfect symmetry, made possible by the bisection of a stand of tall trees by the rich green of the drive that dips then climbs towards the fountain at the front of the house that itself displays symmetry of windows either side of the central, front door.

'What a great approach to your house George.'

'It's further than you might think. We'll take the buggy.'

I follow George to a doorless shed that is tucked away amongst the nearby trees. 'I often use this to get from the house to this part of the garden. I use the trailer to carry tools and plants to where I want to work. Hop in. It's fairly light and the drive is firm so it doesn't mess up the grass with my to-ing and fro-ing. Let's go.'

George presses a button and a quiet electric motor begins to propel us towards the dip in the expanse of grass that separates the trees, then up towards the house. There is a similar doorless shed set amongst the trees near the house where George turns off the motor. 'Here we are James, let's go in.'

Our footsteps make a pleasing crunching sound that accompanies the splash of the fountain as we step across sandy-coloured gravel towards the front door of George's splendid house. I can see that it has two storeys as well as a series of windows embedded in the steep slope of the slate, mansard roof. 'It's kind of modelled along the lines of a small French chateau,' says George as he notices me looking up at the roof.

We reach a short flight of stone steps that leads to an impressive, double door. George pushes the left hand half of the door open. 'You can leave your outside shoes there,' says

George as I follow him inside. 'It's strictly bare feet or stocking feet once past the threshold.'

I bend down to untie my laces and add my boots the considerable collection of footwear that is arranged on shelves in the large vestibule. George has removed his gardening boots and has disappeared through the inner double door of the vestibule, leaving one of them open as an invitation to follow him. What am I doing in George Harrison's house, I think to myself as I hesitate, take a deep breath and enter the hall, closing the inner door of the vestibule behind me.

The large hall has a dark wooden floor and is panelled from floor to ceiling in an equally dark wood. The ceiling and cornices are decorated with elaborate white plasterwork which is echoed around the two chandeliers that illuminate the paintings that are suspended from picture rails. I immediately recognise the style of Vincent van Gogh: a painting of John Lennon and George Harrison. There is very little by way of natural light that enters the hall directly; this must be the reason, I surmise, that the lights are on at this time of day.

I am staring at painted portraits of all four members of the Beatles, hanging in a neat row on the wall opposite the front door when I hear George's voice. 'In here man,' he says as he opens a door to my left to a room at the front of the house and leans into the hall. I had already heard the muffled sound of a piano being played when I entered the hall; its sound is now able to swirl and spread through the open door, filling the hall with a calm melody.

'Come on in; there's someone here who would like to talk to you.'

I have barely taken two steps through the door before my eyes are drawn to an immediately recognisable figure seated at a white grand piano that is placed near the central window of the three windows that flood light into the large room.

'I think you know who this is,' says George as John Lennon looks up from his music sheets, stops playing and extends his right hand.

'This is a great honour Mister Lennon,' I say as I return his firm handshake. 'This place continues to hold surprises. Some time ago, I met George in the garden, and now you. No-one back there in the other place would believe me if I could tell them about meeting you two.'

'Call me John, man. You'd be locked up for being mad.'

'I'll make some coffee,' says George. 'Make yourself at home.'

John and I occupy two of the leather armchairs that are arranged around a low, marble-topped table near the elegant fireplace. He is dressed in black jeans, a black tee-shirt and a dark blue jacket; his hair is long and he is wearing a pair of the round-rimmed spectacles that were usually associated with John Lennon.

'George has his gardening ... I compose and paint.' John offers this information as if he has anticipated my first question.

'I see that you've got a Vincent van Gogh: the one of George and you.'

'An easily recognised style,' says John.

'I too have one, at least I did until my Guardian borrowed it. I feel a bit of a fraud owning it to be honest. The other portraits in the hall: are they yours?' I ask.

'Yeah, the others are mine ... did two of them from memory of course. Paul and Ringo still going strong?'

'I'm not sure what Ringo is doing these days, but Paul has a band and still tours. His set usually includes lots of Beatles' songs. The first time I saw Paul and his band, I remember how thrilling it was to hear those songs. Everyone in the audience knew the words, even young kids. At one concert there was this girl in front of us - she must have been no morel than ten years old - she was dancing and singing along to everything.

'Paul usually does a warm and generous tribute to you and to George. Some people might think that this is a bit corny ... I don't, he means it. Paul is a "sir" by the way.'

'Sir Paul!' says John. 'I'm glad he's fronting a band and doing our songs. Despite the breakup of The Beatles and all of the post-breakup stuff, we all had some good times.'

'And you wrote great songs ... and George did. I'll never forget Elvis singing *All Things Must Pass* ... never.'

'You were there that night,' says George as he places a tray of coffee things on the table. 'We often get together in that bar and have a good time. You must know someone in the know?'

'It was my first day here. I guy who I used to work with called Jim ... he died suddenly. He was only in his thirties. A huge shock. Anyway,

JIm took me. A gig to die for. I thought that I was in heaven when I saw who was in the band. Oh, perhaps I am in heaven?

'What a thing to tell everyone back home ... back there I mean, if I had the chance. Something else I could be locked up for.'

'Best not to tell anyone then,' says John.

'You could tell yourself though,' says George as he pours coffee. 'Help yourself to milk and sugar.'

'Well that's the brief news about Paul - sorry, Sir Paul - and Ringo,' says John. 'What else have we left behind?'

'Do you really want to know?' I ask. 'Here we are in this peaceful place where everything is well-organised; no-one goes without anything; there is no crime, not that I'm aware of anyway; no wars ... "nothing to kill or die for" to quote one of your greatest lyrics John, and "no religion too". Your imagination turned out right then; how about that? Here, I mean You also imagined "all the people living life in peace" in the same song. Sadly, the world that you wished for and *imagined* in your song is as far away as it ever was for those that we have left behind, further probably. So, do you really want to know?'

'I told John about nine-eleven says George. 'It happened a couple of months before I got here. It was painful to tell John about it, but I think that he would like to know more from you.' George retreated into the depths of his armchair and I waited for John to speak.

'What led up to that horrendous event?' John asks me.

'I'm just trying to think; it's more than ten years ago now. I think that it was largely a reaction to American foreign policy in the Middle East. Nothing specific, if I recall ... it just came out of the blue, literally. It was such a beautiful, sunny morning in New York. I can't thing of anything specific that led up to it; it was a reaction to American policy by ultra extremists.

'Knocking down the twin towers was a massive shock. Nothing like this had been perpetrated by terrorists before. I remember that I had started a new job the day before - nine-eleven was on a Tuesday; there hardly seemed any point in going to work any more. The world would never be the same again.

'George Bush's response, the American response that is - he was president at the time - was to declare a "war on terror". As a result, Afghanistan was invaded on the basis that it was a hot-bed of terrorism. A coalition of forces from the USA, the UK and elsewhere are still there now, fighting the Taliban. There seems no end to it. Iraq was invaded a couple of years later, in two thousand and three.

'The whole Middle East situation is mess John, as it ever was. Now that Islamic terrorists have replaced Irish republican terrorists as the new threat, we were living in the constant fear of terror attacks from them since the Irish Republican Army has given up its terror campaign. So, the scourge of the latter part of the twentieth century - the threat of terrorist attacks - continues into the twenty first century with no sign of a let up. It's all very depressing; an uncertain world awaits those that we have left behind.

'Oh, I've just remembered another line from the same song John: "Imagine there's no heaven". Perhaps that line is the odd one out, given where we are? Where the hell are we anyway?' Neither John or George answer: they are both smiling enigmatically at me from the depth of their armchairs. I decide to plough on.

'A few years after George died - sorry, that sounds a bit odd what with you sitting there George. A few years after George *left*, we had a terror attack perpetrated by "home-grown" terrorists in that three of them were of Pakistani descent and lived in the UK. They were from the Asian community in the UK; they lived in Leeds. I forget where the other one lived; he was a Jamaican, so how he got mixed up in it is a mystery to me. He must have become a radicalised Muslim somehow. So, three of the group of terrorists were young, British Asians, the sons of immigrants from the Indian sub-continent, and the fourth a young Jamaican man.

'Anyway, on the seventh of July two thousand and five, these four young men travelled to London from Yorkshire, I think, and arrived in time for the morning rush hour. I think that their original plan was to board four underground trains and travel north, south, east and west and detonate their bombs in a co-ordinated attack. Something must have happened at the last minute because as events unfolded, they detonated their suicide bombs on three trains and the fourth suicide bomber exploded his on a London bus in Tavistock Square. More than fifty people were killed, including the bombers, in the name of what: some twisted notion of Islam? I feel sick in my stomach just thinking about those desperate people trapped in underground train carriages.'

John and George listen attentively while I attempt to explain further the rise of Islamic-based terrorism around the world. I mention a few other instances of terror attacks in various countries, merely to underline how widespread such incidents had become.

'You can't think about it all the time though,' I say, 'otherwise you wouldn't leave the house to go to work or whatever. We had almost become used to the ever-present threat in some bizarre way. People just want to get on with their lives in the hope that the threat will eventually recede. Perhaps it will; I don't know. When I left, wars were raging in the Middle East and it seemed to me that there were few signs of peace breaking out.'

'"Imagine there's no religion ..."', says George, slightly mis-quoting from John's song as he leans forward and pours himself another cup of coffee.

'If only people listened to your warning John,' I say.

'We were only a rock and roll band; why would anyone take any notice?' says John.

'But you must admit that there was a feeling of optimism in the sixties and the early seventies; you guys were part of it. What I have left behind is a sense of pessimism; that's how I felt anyway. War and terror: it goes on as it has for ages. I can't help but be pessimistic about the place that I have left behind.

'So there we are. Wars in the Middle East and the terror attacks that I've told you about are dominant features of the life that I've left. You are both better off out of it.'

The room is quiet, save for the clinking of cups and saucers and the creaking of leather armchairs.

'Thanks for filling us in man,' says John. 'Mankind has a knack of failing to live in peace; what you've told us is not surprising but is very sad.'

'I'm sorry to be the bringer of gloomy news, but you did ask. I could tell you a lot more, but I think you have got the message about what has been going on recently.'

'Yeah, and there is nothing that we can do about it,' says George. 'We tried to change things in our own small way when we were there, but music and art can't put a stop to terrorism and war. Only people can do that. And it doesn't seem as if that is likely to happen back there any time soon. We can only wait for more arrivals in the future who might bring us better news that you have. I feel sad for the loved ones that we have left behind.'

'Just to continue on another gloomy note: you'll love this one because nothing like this happened in our lifetime - we are all about the same age. The financial sector almost brought the world to its knees. There was an almost complete failure in the money markets. This was in about two thousand and eight. There was a run on at least one bank in the United

States and one in the UK. A number of banks on both sides of the Atlantic were bailed out by both governments to the tune of several tens of billions of pounds and dollars. What followed was the largest economic recession since the nineteen twenties. A case of the ruthless market trampling all over the planet!'

'Good God,' says George. 'Aren't you glad that you are here and not there?'

'Of course, even though I don't understand what or where this place is or how I got here.'

'Don't think about it,' says John. 'Just accept it; that's all there is to it. We are here, this place exists ... accept it.

'Something like a perfect society has been created here, a Utopia if you like. Don't ask me how, I don't know, but it has. All material needs are met because there are enough resources for everyone so there is no need to steal from anyone. Therefore there is no crime. Everyone has land and a place to live. There is no need to *take* land from anyone; therefore there is no war. There is no need to crave for an afterlife that is better than the one we started with. This is it; therefore there is no religion. Think how many problems that solves. This all might seem simplistic to a newcomer such as you James, but that's my reading of this place since I left the other place over twenty years ago. You've been here only for a few months James. Try to accept that this place shows how mankind *can* live.'

'Thanks John,' I say. 'I'll try.'

'Use your time here to do and achieve the things you didn't or couldn't do back there,' says George. 'We continue with our music. I work in the garden and John composes music and paints. So art in all of its forms is the most important thing in our lives. We're content.'

'I've started writing,' I say. 'I've always wanted to write but my job didn't leave me any time for it.'

'There you are then, you are on your way to achieve something that you've always wanted to do,' says George.

'My Guardian suggested that I write a memoir of my time here.'

'That would make interesting reading back there,' says George.

'No-one would believe it though,' I say.

'Keep up the writing,' says John. 'It'll help you to accept your new life. *You'll* believe it.'

'Thanks for your time, both of you and for the coffee George. It's been great meeting you in person John, different from watching you play on stage that time when I arrived here.

'By the way George, Martin Scorsese - the famous film director - oh, you probably know that ... sorry. Anyway, he has made a film about you. It was great to see something dedicated to you, although there are scenes of the Beatles together in the first part; the second part is dedicated to your post-Beatles time. It was lovely to hear your wife and your son talking about you. He is the spitting image of you George. I did a double take when he appeared; he is *so* like you.

'Sorry to mention your wife Olivia. She is lovely. I didn't mean to upset you by reminding you of her and your son Dhani. Sorry.'

'That's alright James. I think about them every day.'

'At some point in the film, Dhani said that he had a dream about you and he asked you where you were. You answered "I'm still here." Dhani is a very spiritual man, like you. He seems a lovely guy. You can be proud of him.'

'I miss them both, but there are lots of memories to keep me going. See you at the diner next time,' says George. 'No doubt your man will get to know when we put a band together for a one-nighter. We like to keep these events quiet and spontaneous for obvious reasons.'

We all stand up; I shake John and George by the hand. 'I'll find my way out. Thanks again.

'Before I go, I must tell you this. It's kind of positive after all the gloomy things that I've told you about. We had the Olympics in London in two thousand and twelve. During the closing ceremony, a choir of adults sang John's *Because* and George's *Here Comes the Sun* and a choir of children from Liverpool sang John's *Imagine* followed by a video of John - on a huge screen - singing the end of the song. This was set up by Yoko, I believe. It was a lovely moment; the words of *Imagine* being used to reinforce the message of togetherness and peace - really appropriate to the closing of the Olympics. So you see, your songs still mean something.'

'That's great,' says John. 'How is Yoko?'

'She is much more respected as a serious artist these days than in the early days. I'm not familiar with her stuff, but she is still working on her art. She would be proud to know that you paint John.

'And George, a few years ago Olivia entered a garden in the Chelsea Flower Show. Apparently, the Queen remarked to Olivia that everyone loved George and he is much missed.'

'Very sweet of Her Majesty. See you in the garden man,' says George as he carries the tray of coffee things across the hall to the sound of John playing the same melody that I heard on the way in. I put my boots on and close the front door behind me. George was quoted as saying that he felt that he was on the wrong planet unless he was in his garden at Friars Park: he is surely on the right planet now.

A clamour of birdsong fills the air as I head for home across George's garden; the walk gives me time to think about my visit this morning. Harmony and a lightness of being exist here, in this place. Why, then, was it so difficult to overcome the obstacles to achieving a state of peaceful agreement and co-operation in my former world? Apart from blaming mankind's folly and recklessness, I have no ready answer to this troubling question. I vow to take the advice of John Lennon and others that I have met here and live for the here and now; I can't do anything about the there and then.

Chapter Eight

Questo è un Uomo (This is a Man)

The day I meet the climber dawns cool and sunny, despite the gradual onset of autumn. I leave my house shortly after dawn, with the intention of spending the day walking a circular route across the dales and fells that surround where I live. The village does not stir as I close my front door quietly and make for the footpath that starts behind the village hall. The rough track rises quickly and steeply through trees to emerge on open moorland above the village. Wisps of early-morning mist are suspended over the village as if a giant silk shawl has been shredded and cast over the dale, leaving holes for roofs and chimneys to poke through. Other pieces of the shawl have been caught in the tops of trees below me and have sunk down to reveal a wood that appears to grow out of a cloud rather than rooted on solid ground.

    I sit on the large boulder that has provided me with a suitable resting place on the many occasions that I have taken this walk and look down over our quiet village and think about my eventful life in this idyllic, bucolic Arcadia. The grass around my walking boots is damp from this morning's dew, so I place my rucksack on another boulder to keep it dry. The rock where I sit marks the junction of four, well-marked paths: the one that I have just climbed up from the village and three others that span out across the fells towards distant peaks or adjacent dales. I know most of these paths and have decided to make for the highest peak for today's walk. The route there and back usually takes a few hours, so I left the house early, fully-kitted out in walking gear with rain-proof clothes and food and drink in my rucksack.

I always stop at this place to sit and look down at the village, even if I have planned only a short walk. Today this mandatory pause, enables me to revel in the view of the dale that is my home and reflect on my good fortune to have been sent to this mysterious place. Have I been reincarnated or have I been sent to some sort of half-way house that is half-way to what: to an eternal life; to the hereafter? Is it some form of afterlife where I meet some of my heroes of my first, real life? Do I exist in some other dimension unknown and undetected in my first life? Or has my mind been uploaded to a virtual world: I haven't considered this possibility as yet? Or is it something else that is completely outside my meagre and feeble comprehension? I don't know the answer to any of these questions, not the least of which is: what follows *this* existence? I only know that I am here, sitting on this boulder, looking at this view and that I must maintain this journal. Perhaps *this* is reality and my past life has been a dream. My troubled thoughts are further complicated by the recurring dream that I had again last night. The dream is becoming more vivid and real; this time, I woke up in a state of anxiety, not knowing where I would find myself. I decide to talk to Kal about my disturbing dream; it might mean something, something that I don't want to find out.

I decide that it is time to put these thoughts to one side not for the first time, shoulder my rucksack and start for the Pike as today's destination is known locally. The rocky path to the top of the Pike mostly follows the beds of dry streams or is marked by a series of wooden posts across open moorland to guide the walker across the grassy slopes of the fells. The route to the top of the Pike is regarded as the most challenging walk that starts in my village. Consequently. I usually have the route to myself although I have met intrepid walkers on occasions going in the opposite direction to me, affording a brief acknowledgement rather than a conversation.

After about two hours of generally toiling in an upwards direction, I decide to stop for a short rest. I am now high enough above our long, narrow dale to see the next two villages further along the valley from my own. The mist has disappeared and sky is clear and blue save for a few streaky clouds of white. Lapwings glide and dive, their calls the only sound up here on the high moors. The mid-morning air is cool on my hands and face, suggesting a promise of a change in the season. Since I have lived in the village, I have taken the apparent perpetual summer for granted. Today is the first day that I notice a subtle change in the weather. The slopes of the fells opposite my resting place show a patchwork of greens and browns, redolent of autumn at home in my former life. I mean to ask Kal about the change of seasons: what does it indicate; the well-understood rotation of a planet in some solar system? I haven't given this aspect of my present existence much thought but have submitted unquestioningly to an endless summer.

I shoulder my rucksack again and promise myself lunch at the top without any more breaks for a rest. The path to the top from here follows a series of cairns and wooden finger posts across the steep, wide fell. The dale that I left earlier this morning is almost invisible from up here, its place taken by rolling moorland in all directions that dips here and there to give the merest suggestion of a dale hidden far below.

After another two hours of brisk walking since my previous resting place, the distant and fuzzy outline of the top of the Pike begins to take on its familiar rocky profile. The final approach to the top flattens out to some extent until an almost vertical wall of rock is reached. This particular rock face is popular amongst rock climbers, most of whom reach it from the adjacent dale to mine because the walk to it is shorter and easier than the route from my village. The less ambitious amongst us can reach the final cairn on the top by skirting around the base of the rock face to take the easy route up a scree slope to reach the grassy plateau atop the cliff.

I often spot climbers replete with their mysterious equipment that dangles and clanks as they inch slowly up the face of the cliff. Rock climbers usually work in teams of two or more when attempting this particular climb. Today, as I work my way round to the left of the base of the cliff, I notice a lone climber almost half-way up. He or she - I can't tell from here - must be very experienced: it is unusual to see a climber on his or her own. I scramble up the scree and wait for the climber to reach the top the hard way.

I drop the obligatory stone on the cairn that marks the top of the Pike and settle down against a large boulder. I am out of the wind here and have a grand view of the fells that spread out before me. A distant cleft in the folds of land hints at the presence of the dale where I live; other dips in the moors suggest other dales that slice into the high pastures and meadows. Unseen to the north is the desert strip that lies between the dales and fells and the coast. The familiarity of this view from this slab of rock never fails to fill me with delight and a sense of well-being. Is this what immortality or eternity feels like; is this what an alternative dimension looks like?

There is no-one with me to share such searching questions, so I dismiss them in favour of the peace and joy of the immediacy and splendour of the high fells. Then I remember the climber. I often have the top of the Pike to myself; this time, I have my invisible companion.

My vantage point is several feet from the top of the cliff. I decide to stay where I am rather than stand at the top and peer down at the climber; such an action might be disturbing or intimidating. He or she might not have noticed me ascend the cliff from its side path, so the sudden appearance of another human being might provide an element of unwanted surprise.

I pour myself a cup of coffee from the vacuum flask that is stowed in my rucksack and lean against my rocky backrest, nursing the metal cup in both hands and wait for the climber to appear above the top of the cliff.

I don't have long to wait. After a few sips of coffee, the climber's head and shoulders appear. He is looking below him, concentrating on his final few footholds, and doesn't see me at first. All that I can see of the climber's head is the top of a grey, wooly hat. He - for this is a man - seems surprised when he looks up.

'I hope that I didn't give you a shock,' I say.

'Hello,' comes the reply, 'I wasn't expecting anyone to be here.'

'I came up the easy way. I saw you from below. You were about half-way up so you didn't see me go round to get here before you.'

The climber is on his feet now, gathering up ropes and other pieces of equipment. He drops a small backpack on the ground and sits on a rock a few feet to my right.

'Mind if I stay?' I say to him. 'I don't wish to disturb your peace.'

'Of course, please stay. I don't mind at all.'

'Would you like some coffee? I have another cup.'

'Thank you, I would like that.'

'Sugar?'

'If you have some. You even carry sugar?'

'Sugar yes, but I don't bother with milk.'

'Then one sugar will be fine, thank you.'

While I pour the climber a cup of coffee, he removes his hat and replaces his climbing shades with a pair of almost circular, broad-rimmed glasses.

'Don't get up,' he says as he walks towards me and reaches down for the cup.

'Your English is excellent, Mr. Levi,' I say as the climber returns to his chosen rock. As soon as I saw the climber without his hat, I recognised the wave of grey hair that threatens to either roll forwards like a wave or recede to reveal even more of his high forehead.

'I couldn't help but recognise you, I hope you don't mind. I've seen many photographs of you.'

Even though he is seated, I could see that my companion is slightly built and quite short in stature. He looks at me over his cup. Primo Levi's face is as beautiful as I expected from reading about him and from watching film clips on the Internet. It is true what I have read: his eyes *are* soft and serene. I could hardly stop myself staring at one of my heroes. Here sits Primo Levi, a great writer, a surviver of Nazi concentration camps, sharing my flask of coffee.

'Not at all. I'm not often recognised these days. How is it that you know who I am?'

'Oh, photographs mostly. There's a very good one on the dust jacket of a biography of you that I've read. There are quite a few photographs of you inside the book as well.

'Incidentally, I thought that rock climbers climb in a group, for safety and so on. I've never seen a rock climber on his own.'

'My friends and I have climbed this cliff several times. We have left enough pitons on the route to clamp to, so it is safe to climb it alone. I've got a ground anchor.'

'A ground anchor?'

'The rope is anchored to a rock at the foot of the cliff. I pull the rope up with me and attach it to the rock every few metres. The rope is slack if I pull it up but it will tense if I fall off. I will only fall as far the attachment point that is immediately below me.'

'It sounds very technical and looks rather scary.'

'It is perfectly safe as long as you know what you are doing. It's easier to have a ground anchor than a top one if you are on your own. When I finish the route, I can climb down and retrieve my rope. Today I will go down the way you came up. I have to come up here to fix a top anchor. A ground anchor saves me the trouble of scrambling up here to make a top anchor only to go back down to start climbing. Thank you for the coffee. You've never tried rock climbing?'

'Oh no, I've no head for heights. I just couldn't do it. I admire your skill in being able to climb solo.'

'Solo with a rope. True solo climbing is without a rope. I couldn't do that.'

'I remember reading in your biography that you used to go walking in the mountains in your native Italy. I don't remember reading anything about rock climbing though.'

'I only started it when I came here. As you can see, there are no mountains here abouts, not like in Italy, just hills and moors.

Very pleasant for walking as you know. So, I started rock climbing with a group of friends. We usually climb together - the safest way - but today I just liked the idea of an easy, familiar solo climb.'

'Easy! That vertical cliff is easy?'

'It may be vertical, but it has lots of slits and knobbly sections that are good for hands and feet to grip on. It's not as smooth as it might appear from a distance. Smooth is no good for rock climbing; we have to have something to get hold of and put our feet on, even if it is only small. You'd be surprised what one can put one's weight on. As long as I can keep on climbing at my age without fear of falling, then I am happy.'

'Well, Mr. Levi, you look fit. It must be doing you good.'

'Please call me Primo.' Primo Levi stands, extends his hand and walks towards me. I too stand and grasp the little man's hand in mine. This is the hand that wrote elegantly-crafted books about how he survived Auschwitz, how he overcame the experience and bore witness to it in his writing; this hand also wrote poetry, fiction and books that narrated his scientific and literary life. I dare not squeeze the tiny hand too much for fear of damaging its ability to pass words from his mind to the page. 'It is a pleasure to meet a fellow walker', he says.

'I wondered if you would be here, in this place I mean. It is an honour to meet you.'

We return to our respective rocky seats and sit facing one another.

'Please don't be concerned. I'm not going to ask you the usual questions. I remember reading somewhere you said that "people always ask me the same questions". I've read many of your books so there is no need for me to ask you about Auschwitz. I've read your account. You survived and you bore witness for the benefit of all of mankind.'

Primo smiles. 'A biography? What does it say about my death?'

'We don't have to go into that Primo, only if you really want to know. Presumably it brought you here more than twenty years ago. I've been here about six months,' I say in an attempt to divert Primo Levi from discussing his apparent suicide and shift the focus to my own departure from our previous existence.

'We have at least three things in common Primo. Firstly, constant worry about an ageing and sick mother.'

Primo Levi looks away for a moment and distracts his thoughts by rummaging in his back pack.

'Did you find that it dominated your life?' Primo asks.

'When my mother was well, I felt free. When she was ill, I just wanted her health problems to go away and stop impinging on my life ... I felt guilty and selfish. She depended on me and that made me feel that my freedom was lost to some extent. I don't know what I expected: that she would simply grow old and stay well. How unrealistic can that be and how selfish?'

'What happened to her?'

'She survives me. She is well into her nineties. I wonder how she is coping with the grief? No mother wants to lose her son.'

'I heard that my mother survived me by a few years.'

'That's correct Primo. Your mother survived you by four years. She died in nineteen ninety one, aged ninety four.'

'To die before one's parent. I didn't expect that.'

'Me neither. My mother is still going strong, well she was when I left anyway. Her sister once said to me that my mother will outlive all of us in the family. Looks like my aunty might be right.'

'And the other things?'

'Other things?'

'You said that we had at least three things in common.'

One of the many things that I had taken away from reading Carole Angier's wonderful biography of Primo Levi is that he was reputed to be a good listener. Even when dark thoughts pressed down on him, he would put his depression to one side and listen to the troubles of others. Now he is taking the time to listen to the ramblings of a complete stranger on the top of a mountain.

'Oh yes, the second thing. I also was diagnosed with an enlarged prostate. When you had yours almost three decades ago, they must have been keen on surgery. In my case, the enlargement was regarded as benign. They are more enlightened these days: there is no need for surgery in most cases of an enlarged prostrate.'

'I hated the whole experience. In hindsight, my operation probably wasn't necessary. The aftermath contributed to my depression.

'Would you like some fruit cake?' says Primo, with a sudden change of subject.

'No thanks Primo, I've got some lunch in here.' We both proceed to ferret about in our back packs for food and remain silent for a while.

'One more thing, the third thing,' I say, between mouthfuls. 'I read somewhere that you bought an Apple computer in the early nineteen eighties. It must have been a very early model?'

'It was an Apple Two-c. I learnt how to word-process and used it to write some of my books.'

'You should see what Apple computers look like now, nearly thirty years later. The communicators that they give us here are similar to a device known as the Apple iPhone™. I had an iPhone™ back there; they play music too.'

'Music?'

'Yes. The mobile 'phone market is huge back there. An early computer user such as you would have loved the technology that you have missed ... well, I'm only guessing; you might not have wanted to be contactable by mobile 'phone *all* of the time. All you had to do was switch it off if you didn't want to be contacted. It was nice to be able to listen to music to and from work on the train though. The iPhone™ came with earphones. There are several manufacturers of mobile 'phones, but Apple was the first to combine the mobile 'phone with a portable music device. As you know, Apple was amongst the first of several companies to manufacturer a personal computer and Apple are still around today. It is just about the richest company in the world. Steve Jobs was sorely missed; I understand that he is here somewhere.

'How interesting that you got into personal computers so early in their development. It was the same for me. I wrote my first technical report on a personal computer in nineteen eighty two. It was a matter of learning how to use word processing software very quickly.'

'What was your job, your career?' asks Primo.

'I started out as a research chemist, like you: a chemist. I didn't go on to make a career out of it as you did. I gave up chemistry after I finished my doctorate and moved into computing as soon as I could. I guess that I took a chance and switched academic subjects.   I was involved in software engineering until I arrived here.'

'You are right: we do have a few things in common.'

'Purely coincidental. I'm not a great writer like you.'

'Thank you; you are very kind. Towards the end of my life I feared that my writing would be forgotten.   I thought that the younger generation wouldn't want to be told about the Holocaust; they seemed bored with it. Also ..., ' Primo paused and sighed deeply, 'also, I and some of my fellow survivors struggled to keep up with responding to Holocaust deniers.'

'For someone like you, a survivor of the Lager, who testified so eloquently and humanely, encountering revisionists and deniers must have been so hard, so painful For the life of me, I've never understood deniers.   Pure ignorance Primo ... naked ignorance.'

'There must be more to it than ignorance,' says Primo.

'How can there be? For example, I have had the misfortune to confront a denier only once. "There's masses of evidence." I said to him. "Have you read Primo Levi or do you know what happened to Anne Frank?" "Who is Primo Levi?" he said. My case rests Primo.'

Primo says no more on the subject and busies himself unwrapping a sandwich.

'By the way, I read a lovely quote that you made about Anne Frank ... something about being able to take in the suffering of one person - Anne Frank - because mankind would be incapable of taking in the suffering of all the others who perished in the concentration camps. I think I understand what you meant by that.'

'I survived but, of course, Anne and her family did not. Her's was but one tragedy amongst countless others. We have Anne's diary as a testament to her young life and her hopes that were cruelly extinguished before the war came to an end.'

'And we have *your* books Primo. Both Anne Frank and you testified; this is *so* important for the generations that we have left behind.'

'There is no more that I can do about it now; it has been left behind. We are both living in a perfect place now. My health was rather poor towards the end of my life, but here I am rock climbing!'

'Good for you Primo. You deserve this better life. You did humanity a great service through your writing; you taught us a great deal about what it was like to be sent to a concentration camp and how you survived it and returned home. We needed accounts like yours to help us understand the mentality of the Nazis and what it meant to be persecuted merely for being a Jew. The legacy of your writing is of great importance to people like me who were born just after the end of the second world war.

'I don't know what I've done to deserve this new life though.'

'It must have been something,' says Primo.

'Well, I think that I will get going ... collect my rope from below and return home. Which way do you go down?'

'My village is down there.' I point in the direction of my hidden dale. 'My name is James, by the way.'

'I go that way.' Primo points in the opposite direction. He has gathered up his equipment and his back pack and extends his hand again.

'We will meet again, somewhere in these hills I am sure,' he says as he shakes my hand in farewell. 'I have enjoyed our little chat James.'

'The next time we meet Primo, I would like to ask you something. I forget where I read this, but you predicted a clash between Islam and the West. There's a great deal that I could tell you about this, things that have happened since you came here. I was merely wondering what led you to such a prediction. You were right in what you foresaw, the consequences have been horrendous. Perhaps we can talk about it some time.'

'I have heard things, nine eleven in particular. What has happened fills me with great sadness. We might talk about it one day. For now, I must be off. Goodbye.'

I watch Primo descend the steep scree slope that I came up earlier this morning. Before the upper part of his body disappears from view, he turns towards me. 'I suppose they think that I committed suicide?'

'I think they do, Primo,' I call out to him before he disappears out of sight.

I let a few minutes pass for the climber to collect the remainder of his equipment from the foot of the cliff before I venture to the edge and peer over. I can see the distant figure of Primo Levi striding away from my vantage point. He stops, turns and waves in my direction. I wave back and continue to watch him until the contours of the high fells swallow him up.

Chapter Nine

In Their Footsteps

I wrestled with the notion of arranging a meeting between Primo and Anne for several days after my encounter with Primo on the Pike, my mind wavering back and forth between my feelings for Anne's privacy and that of her family and my impetuosity - or was it vanity? - in wishing Anne to meet the man who is quoted as saying: "... Anne Frank moves us more than the countless others who suffered just as she did but whose faces have remained in the shadows." What would be gained if I brought these two people together: a survivor and a victim of the Holocaust, apart from stilling the torment in my mind? Primo solved the problem for me when we met for the second time.

Our second meeting occurred a few days after the first: I was on my way up the Pike and Primo was on his way down.

'Hello Primo. You're coming down into my dale this time.'

'I'm on my way to Morlham, so I've decided to go there from the station in your village. How nice to meet you, I thought that we might meet around here one day.'

We talked about the weather and the condition of the path to the summit of the Pike for a few minutes.

'It is very slippery on the scree up there,' indicated Primo. 'Be careful at the top.'

'Thanks, I will.

'Primo, can I ask you something? I'm sorry that this is out of the blue, half way up a mountain ... but can I ask you ...?'

'Of course. What is it?'

'This is going to sound a bit strange, out here asking you this.'

'Please go on. We might not bump into one another for a while.'

'Thank you, alright then. Do you ever meet - here I mean - any victims of Auschwitz, anyone who died in Auschwitz or Birkenau?'

Primo was silent for a while, his gaze turned from me towards the path and the descent to my village. A soft breeze caught our faces as Primo looked directly at me again.

'I *could* do, I could have met several victims and survivors in this place but I choose not to. I can understand why you ask, but I ask you to try to understand why I avoid such encounters. My Guardian keeps me insulated from such things, so I have avoided it.

'I will tell you about it one day. One day, we will sit down at the summit of the Pike and we can talk about Auschwitz; we can talk about the survivors and the victims.'

'Thank you Primo, it is very kind of you to answer my rather abrupt question. I'm sorry that I reminded you about your past. I imagine that the last thing that you want is for interfering people like me reminding you about your past.'

'Please don't concern yourself James. I can never forget my experience in Auschwitz. That would be impossible. The memory cannot be erased; it will always be with me. Even in this place, it is always with me, in the background but always there like an itch that goes away momentarily but returns anew. I have learnt to live with it. I am able to push such memories away and control them. Being here helps of course.'

'By the way Primo. I visited Auschwitz and Birkenau. I thought about you during my visit. I thought about you and how you survived. I felt that I was following in your footsteps as we were guided around the camps.'

'I am glad that you visited that place,' said Primo. 'We have more to talk about now.'

'Thanks again Primo.

'Do you have a train timetable? You'll probably be in time for the two o'clock train to Morlham.

'I would very much like it if you would pay me a visit the next time you are in my village. My house is the third one along from the village shop. I'd be honoured if you would visit.'

'You can be assured that I will. Until then.'

Primo Levi turned away from me and continued on his way along that path that descends the Pike and leads to my village.

❅

Primo's assertion that he had not wanted to meet any victims of the camps settled the matter: there would be no meeting between two witnesses of the horror of the Nazi concentration camps for the time being. I *did* want to tell Anne that I had visited Auschwitz and Birkenau. I simply had to still the turmoil in my mind by telling Anne that I had followed in her footsteps and walked the same paths that she and her family had taken. My mind burned with the memory of my visit, trying to imagine their hunger and suffering at the hands of the Nazis, striving to understand what it must have been like to have been imprisoned in that place.

I worried about how Anne would react, I fretted about whether our friendship would be damaged. Nevertheless, the strong desire to tell Anne led me to decide to take a risk and tell her of my visit the next time we met in George's garden.

An opportunity presented itself on the Sunday following my second encounter with Primo. Despite the inclement weather that promised showers between patches of weak autumn sun, I went for a walk in George's garden in the hope that Anne would be in the summerhouse, in spite of the slight chill in the air that marked the turning of the seasons.

My footsteps on the lakeside path made Anne look up from her work and wave.

'Writing today? Are you sure that this is the weather for working outdoors? Does your family worry that you might catch cold?'

'Oh James, don't fuss so. You sound like one of them, my family I mean.'

'Sorry Anne. It's just that ...'

'I know ... you mean well; you are kind and thoughtful. I'm glad to have a friend such as you. You can make a fuss of me if you like.

'Anyway, I'm finishing a short story for the local paper. It should be in next week,' said Anne and she put down her pen and stretched her arms wide in an inaudible yawn.

'I'm looking forward to reading it. I could never do short stories. I'm not much good at long stories, come that that, but I'm trying to record my experiences here as best I can, as you know.

'Don't let me stop you. I was passing and I thought: "Sunday afternoon; Anne might be in the summerhouse." And here you are.'

'I don't mind being interrupted. It is always so lovely to see you, to talk to you about things.'

'Anne, there's something that I have been meaning to tell you for some time now. I have to get this off my chest but I'm afraid to find out how you will react. I don't want to spoil our friendship.'

'Oh how mysterious and serious. What is it James?' Anne placed her elbows on the table, rested her chin on her clasped hands and looked intently at me.

I looked down at the table, unable to meet the gaze of her large, dark eyes. 'The fact is Anne, the thing that I've been meaning to tell you is that in my former life, I visited Auschwitz. I'd read your books and I had to see what the place was like, the first camp that you were sent to. It was something that I *had* to do.' I raised my head slowly and met Anne's eyes.

Anne's face was serious and her voice very quiet, a whisper that was barely audible over the rush of the wind amongst the trees that surround the lake. 'We were all there James, as you know. The women were separated from the men, so we never saw father again. They moved Margot and me to another camp and we never saw mother again either.' Now it was Anne who looked down at the table.

'I am so sorry to remind you of this part of your past life. I don't want you to dwell on this any more, but I wanted to tell you because the visit was the most emotional and profound experience of my life, my former life I should say. I wanted to understand what it was like to have been imprisoned in that place.

'When our tour party walked through the women's camp at Birkenau, I thought of you, Margot and your mother. It was a very emotional experience. It suddenly dawned upon me that I might be walking along the same paths amongst the huts, the *same* paths that you passed along. I was overwhelmed. This is why I wanted to tell you. I feel that I have followed in your footsteps.'

Anne looked at me, a single, large tear rolled slowly down her right cheek.

'Oh no, I've made you cry. I am so sorry,' I said with a broken voice. 'I should have kept this to myself. I am so sorry.'

'Don't be James, don't be. Anne wiped her tears away with the flat of her hand and smiled her usual bright smile.

'It's alright. I'm glad you told me, please don't worry yourself.

At home we don't talk about it much. There are times, though, when we may be sitting quietly as a family. We all know what we are thinking. Despite our happy and fulfilled lives here, these thoughts never quite go away altogether. They may recede into the distance as we get further away from them, but we cannot erase them entirely.

'I'm impressed and gladdened that you took the trouble to visit, to try to understand. Not many would.'

'Oh but they do Anne. The site has about one million visitors a year. Just think of it: in ten years, that is ten million people who have been educated and informed about what happened there. Auschwitz and Birkenau are museums, more than that, they are monuments.

'My visit was merely one of many that day, but it had a personal resonance in the realisation that I could have been following in your footsteps. Walking through the women's camp at Birkenau was a very moving experience for me.

'Such an experience can only give the merest insight as to what it must have been like for you and your family. I desperately wanted to try to understand what you went through by *being* there, by going to that place.'

Anne does not take her eyes away from mine. 'Now I see, now I understand why you went there. I'm glad you told me. Don't worry about our friendship, it is stronger than before.' Anne took hold of both my hands in hers and squeezed tightly. 'Everything is alright James. Now we have some shared knowledge and some shared experience of that dreadful place.'

'I'm so relieved Anne. I have a very strong regard for you. Thank you for being so understanding.'

Anne sat back in her chair. 'How does it work, the visit I mean? What happens?'

'Would you let me write it down? I think that I can explain my experience much better if I write it down for you.'

'That's a good idea James. I would really like to know what it was like for you to visit our first camp, as a free man rather than as a prisoner like us.

'Is Auschwitz the only camp that you have visited? Is it possible to visit Belsen, where we ... we died?'

'I haven't visited Belsen. I'm not sure what is left of it, if anything. There is a memorial though. I don't think that I could bear to visit the place where you and your sister suffered so. I found Birkenau difficult enough. The sheer scale of the killings that took place there ... almost impossible to comprehend.

'Shall we go now? What is left of the afternoon sun has almost disappeared behind the fells.'

Anne gathered up her writing materials and slung her leather satchel over her left shoulder as we left the summerhouse. 'Let's walk to the gate to the lane together,' said Anne.

Anne put her arm through mine as we trod familiar paths to the gate that leads from George's garden. No words passed between us until we emerged onto the tree-lined lane.

'Until next Sunday James; same time, same place. Would you bring your account of your visit. I would like to read it.'

'I will,' I said.

Anne gave my left hand a squeeze, smiled and walked quickly away from me along the lane. I stood and watched as the remnants of the late afternoon sun forced its way through gaps in the trees and joined momentary shadows that fell upon the retreating figure. Anne stopped, turned and waved before she disappeared round a bend. I waved back: she knew that I would be waiting, watching over my friend, a remarkable young woman from a remarkable family.

This is what I wrote to show Anne the following Sunday.

❋

Saturday the twenty fourth of November, in the year two thousand and eleven in the reckoning of my old world turned out to be a life-changing day for me, a day that afforded me a vey profound experience. This was the day that I made a trip to Krakow, in Poland, in order to visit Auschwitz I and Auschwitz II (also known as Birkenau).

Upon arrival at Auschwitz I, our tour group is provided with headsets while we await our guide Ania. It feels appropriate to be here on a bitterly cold, late-autumn day. The thin trees that line the perimeter of the site of the concentration camp are almost bare and joyless and seem to reflect the ultimate sadness of this place. The harsh wind shakes the remaining leaves so that they fall to the ground like hot tears shed every autumn for the thousands and thousands of victims who were murdered here. We are wrapped in our private thoughts about what we are here to see as we are joined by Ania who leads us towards the entrance gate above which the words "Arbeit Macht Frei" are picked out in black iron.

To step inside the wire perimeter of Auschwitz I beneath this ominous and mendacious phrase is to pass from one world to another, from the real world to a place that is all too familiar from numerous images. To pass through this gate, as prisoners of the Nazis did, is an affirmation of that familiarity; actually *being* here is something that I immediately feel, physically and emotionally. Stepping through the gate and passing below that bleak symbol of Nazi propaganda in the blink of an eye is a huge step. We have left sanity behind us and have entered the domain of bricks and mortar that is the manifestation of the Final Solution.

Ania talks to us in a quiet voice that we can hear over our headsets. She is young, in her twenties, very knowledgable and conducts the tour with feeling and emotion. I can hear it in her voice, see it in her face. I can feel what she is feeling.

Immediately after passing through that gate, we enter a large area of wide, dusty paths that connect a rectilinear arrangement of dozens of brick-built barracks that housed the innocent people who were transported here from all corners of Europe during the second world war. Ania guides us from block to block and explains, with skill and sensitivity, the displays of photographs and exhibits of bunks and washrooms.

In one room there are huge displays of shoes, glasses and other belongings that were taken from the prisoners. In another room, the vast pile of human hair is almost too much to bear. A group of silent teenagers join me, their faces stricken with grief. It is in this room that I begin to weep inside.

I gaze at a vast heap of suitcases, scanning the names of their owners who probably were forced to pack in a great hurry before they were taken from their homes to be crammed into the notorious trains of cattle trucks that brought them here. The nervous hands that gripped tightly the burdens of worldly goods were soon relieved of them on arrival. Here they are in a dark pile, case upon case, empty of possessions, with the names or initials of their baffled and scared owners stencilled in large letters on the lid, each name a victim, each a silent witness. I don't see it, but Ania tells me later that one of the cases in the exhibit bears the name M. Frank. This battered object might have been Margot's case.

This part of the tour continues through several barrack blocks so that under Ania's expert and measured guidance our tour group builds a picture of life and death in the camp.

By far the hardest part of the tour of Auschwitz I comes at the end, in the final building, the camp's only gas chamber and crematorium. Ania does't speak to us inside this building, she merely points to a hole in the ceiling where the lethal cyanide pellets were dropped into the gas chamber. Ania leaves us to pass through this room and the crematorium beyond on our own: there are no words uttered here and there are none to be found that are adequate.

I spend a few minutes in this awful building, where time elongates heavily and the air hangs with lost memories. My steps are leaden as I pass slowly through this dread space to reach the exit, escape and stand under the sky. It took only a few minutes to murder those selected for extermination, their exit rendered to ash and smoke, the scant remains of their existence. They entered as human beings and left as debris. I too enter as a human being but I am free to emerge as the same being, albeit changed and humbled by the knowledge that filters through the silence of the gas chamber, my shaky composure on the point of destruction.

  The door of the crematorium leads outside into the weak, autumn sunlight, a blessed relief from the gloom of the gas chamber and its accompanying ovens of death. Our tour group are standing outside in silence: Ania lets us regain our equilibrium of mind before taking us to see the gallows where Rudolf Höss, the camp commandant, was hung following his trial shortly after the end of the war. Ania does not gloat or sound triumphant, she merely gives us the facts regarding the death of the Nazi who was responsible for what happened here. It occurs to me, though, that as Höss was being prepared for his death sentence, if he looked to his left he would have been able to see his spacious house and if he looked to his right he would have been in view of the gas chamber. I wondered what final image rested on his mind as his life was squeezed out of him on the gallows.

  A short drive takes us to Auschwitz II, also knows as Birkenau. As our tour bus rounds a bend in the approach road, the infamous entrance gate with its high, central guard tower comes into view. A railway track links the outside world to the interior of the camp by means of an archway beneath the tower. The view of the entrance that we can see would have been denied from the trains of cattle trucks that passed through the archway and on into the camp until they drew to a halt at a siding and platform that stood ready to receive the occupants tumbling out to the shouts of prison guards.

The view from the high tower reveals a vast concentration camp, several times the area of Auschwitz I. The Nazis built Auschwitz II so they could murder Jews more efficiently by means of a number of huge gas chambers and crematoria. The Nazis set fire to the wooden huts of the men's camp when they abandoned Auschwitz in the face of their defeat at the end of the war. All that remains of the scores of barracks is a regular arrangement of brick chimneys that stand like silent sentinels guarding the memories of the condemned men. The brick-built barracks of the women's camp to the left, on the opposite side of the railway track to the men's camp, still stand today.

From where I stand in the guard tower, the fearful symmetry of this treeless place strikes a blow to the senses. The railway track emerges from its archway beneath my feet and points ahead like a deadly arrow to split the camp in two. We descend from the tower and pass through the archway, a bitter wind snatching at our cheeks.

Ania takes us into one of the wooden huts that has been re-constructed at the opening to the men's camp. Conditions would have been much worse in these draughty, wooden barracks than in the brick-built barracks at Auschwitz I. I thought of the suffering of Otto Frank and Primo Levi; they would have been somewhere here in the men's camp before they were liberated at the end of the war. I thought too of the suffering of the countless others who were denied survival.

Ania walks with us deep into Birkenau, following the railway track to the notorious siding where confused Jews faced selection. I glance back towards the entrance gate: this would have been the view, from inside the camp, that deported Jews would have had on arrival at Birkenau, their first sighting of what became known as the "Gate of Death" through which there would be no escape, save for a few souls who survived the selections and were liberated at the end of the war.

We continue our walk to the end of the camp where a starkly impressive monument stands on a wide, brick platform. It is said that the platform is made up of one a half million bricks, one for each murdered victim of Birkenau.

The ruins of one of the huge gas chambers lies near the monument. This structure was dynamited by the Nazis as they faced defeat. Huge blocks of concrete are strewn about and lie untouched and unmoved since 1945 when the Russian army liberated the camp.

We return to the entrance of Birkenau via the women's camp. I am deeply affected by the thought that I might be following the same paths taken by Anne, Margot and Edith Frank when they were imprisoned here and I am almost overcome with the thought of Edith's death in this place and the deaths of Anne and Margot when they were transferred to Bergen-Belsen concentration camp shortly before the end of the war. I look down at my feet on the grass as they move robotically amongst the women's barracks: I feel an overwhelming sadness as I follow what might have been their very footsteps.

Ania bids us farewell at the Gate of Death: "To me this is not a museum, it is about my people, my family." Ania has made this visit more than merely a fact-finding one, but a visit that engaged our heads and our hearts. I steal a final look of admiration at Ania, a young woman charged with the responsibility of telling the world what happened in this place, a young woman who touched our hearts.

There is little talk on the coach on the way back to my hotel in Krakow. I stare blankly out of the window, trying to take in what I have seen and heard today, thinking about the millions of Jews and other people who were murdered in Auschwitz I and Auschwitz II and camps like it. I thought about Otto Frank and Primo Levi who survived Auschwitz and Edith who didn't and I thought about Anne and Margot who were moved from Birkenau concentration camp to Bergen-Belsen concentration camp where they died just before the end of the war.

Now, as I write this, I am lost in a delirious wonder as I think about my new friends, Primo Levi and the Frank family. My heart beats faster and my throat tightens as I think about them all, here in this place, in their new lives.

❇

'Are you really sure that you want to read this Anne? It's a bit factual, but I've tried to put into words what I experienced the day I visited Auschwitz. Are you sure that you want to be reminded about the past?' We were sitting in the summerhouse, as usual, on a Sunday afternoon. A soft autumn rain pattered the roof and glassed the paths around the lake.

'I would like to find out what it was like for you, to be a visitor to that place as a museum. I didn't know it is a museum.'

'More of a monument than a museum. A testament to those who suffered there; "museum" doesn't describe it adequately.' I handed my notebook to Anne.

'I'll go for a walk while you read it. Oh, it's still raining.'

'No, please stay. I won't mind.'

I felt rather self-conscious, sitting opposite Anne, trying to avoid watching her read. Anne didn't look up but she might have been aware of my occasional glances when she tucked her hair behind her ears when it kept falling forwards as she leant over the pages of my notebook.

The rain ceased its gentle interruption on the roof of the summerhouse, so I slipped quietly away to the end of the wooden jetty that led out into the lake from the bank below our meeting place. I sat on the damp wood and dangled my feet towards the surface of the lake. A chill wind pushed wavelets beneath my feet towards the shore: I turned up the collar of my leather greatcoat and waited for Anne. Countless ripples danced below me, mesmerising the stones that lay on the bed of the lake into a shifting pattern that I stared at for many minutes.

Footsteps on the jetty drew me away from my fixed stare of the water below me. Anne sat down next to me, pulled her knees up under her chin and gazed across the lake. The chill wind died down and a watery sun broke through the shifting rain clouds.

'You'll get damp and cold Anne. Your coat is too short to sit on.'

'I wonder if it was Margot's case?' Anne turns to look at me, tears are falling from both eyes. 'Now it's my turn to cry.'

'Anne, I'm so sorry ... sorry to upset you.' Anne takes my proffered handkerchief.

'No, it's alright. It is important for me to know what Auschwitz is being used for now, to educate people so nothing like that ever happens again in our old world.

'It is up to them to see that it doesn't, so that our lives, our sacrifice, wasn't for nothing. Isn't that right James? We shouldn't forget.'

'We can forget in this world, in our new world Anne, but those that we have left behind ... they must never be allowed to forget. There's nothing that we can do about it now: it is their responsibility. You played your part when you wrote your diary. Its rescue by Miep was a miracle. It's over now, you and your family can live in peace and love here in this place, our new world.'

'Can I show your piece of writing to Margot? I don't think that I will show it to the others.'

'Yes, I would like that.'

'It was a very moving account James. Your guide sounds wonderful. Was she young?'

'In her early twenties, I'd say. The baton to bear witness and educate the world has passed to her generation. After more than fifty years, there are precious few survivors left to tell their stories. Ania was wonderful. It is up to her generation to tell the story, a story that must be told in perpetuity.

'Anne, it's beginning to rain again. We should go.'

Anne retreated to the summerhouse at a trot and gathered up her belongings and put them in her shoulder bag.

'I've put your notebook in here,' said Anne as I reached our meeting place. 'Let's see if we can get some tea at George's house.'

I took off my leather coat and wrapped it around Anne's shoulders: it almost reached the ground. Anne gripped my arm: 'You will get so wet,' she said as we set off at a brisk pace in the direction of George's mansion.

I was past caring how wet I would get. I cared much more about protecting and cherishing my young friend, her arm in mine, both of us hoping for a warm fire and tea and cake at the house of George Harrison.

Chapter Ten

Dreams and Doubts

I finally decided to talk to Kal about the same dream that I have had several times during the past few weeks and that has plagued my sleep almost every night for the past week. The most recent occurrences of the dream were highly vivid and seemed to be getting longer or I remembered more of it each time I awoke. I waited until mid-morning after the most recent occurrence of the dream and called Kal.

I picked up my smartphone from the hall dresser where I usually leave it last thing at night and tapped the screen icon that is required to contact Kal's voice mail. Kal's voice breaks in to the recorded message: 'Hello sir,' said a familiar voice, 'what can I do for you this morning?'

'I'll come straight to the point Kal, I'm troubled. Can you come over?'

'I'm in your area. I'll be with you in a few minutes sir. Would you like to put some coffee on?'

'I'll leave the front door open for you.'

I heard Kal's firm knock on my front door as I placed the coffee things on the low table in the front bay window of my living room. 'Come away in Kal, coffee is in the front room.'

My Guardian settled himself into the armchair that he usually sits in when he comes to see me. Kal was dressed elegantly in a light grey suit and matching collarless shirt. His white hair was swept back in immaculate style. Kal is cleaning his silver-framed glasses as I poured him a cup of coffee. He replaced his glasses upon his nose and glanced out of my front window before fixing me with one of his firm and friendly gazes.

Your front garden looks excellent, as usual. Now, what is troubling you on this fine morning?'

'I've taught myself some basic gardening skills while I have been here. I was hopeless at gardening in the other place, but now I'm not too bad. I can grow flowers, as you can see at the front.

'While I have been here, I have done many other things that I wouldn't have had time to do, well ... *before*, if you understand what I mean. For instance, I've learned to play the saxophone and I've joined a creative writing group - as you know - to help me record my experiences here. I'm writing everything down, from the day I arrived at your Arrivals Lounge; I will write up today later.

'I've met many wonderful people and become friends with some of those people who I regarded as my heroes in my former life. Anne Frank and Vincent van Gogh to mention but two. I've met many other wonderful people. I've heard Charles Dickens speak. I've met George Harrison and John Lennon. I've listened to great musicians such as Elvis Presley and Johnny Cash. The list goes on.

'In a word, this place is a kind of Utopia isn't it Kal? For example: there is equality; there are no unfulfilled needs; we are in harmony with nature and its resources. These are just a few of the attributes of this place that define it to be a much better place than where I came from. A fantasy world, if you like. But ... it exists, as far as I can tell. Being here feels real enough, fantasy or no fantasy.'

'We aim to please sir,' said Kal.

'And I can get deep-fried Mars bars, haggis and I can even get Irn Bru™ ice cream! Everything that we Scottish people love about our national cuisine,' I continued.

'*But* ... to be serious ... to be perfectly honest there is something missing though, something I can't quite put my finger on. This *state of being*, as it were, is too perfect. I can't fully articulate how I'm feeling, but something is bothering me. I feel as if I should be *going* somewhere. Or, rather, I feel that I am being pulled somewhere.'

'Ah yes, I've been half-expecting this,' said Kal. 'Have you been having a recurring dream lately?'

'I most certainly have. How did you ... no, I needn't ask. I ought to know by now that you know everything.

'I've been having a very vivid dream lately. It's been going on for a few weeks now. I didn't want to bother you with it ... it's just a dream, or so I thought at first. It's the same dream, but it's getting longer if that makes sense. It has been so vivid lately and *real*. It doesn't occur every night, just every two or three nights. Last night, in particular, was very vivid. It was such a relief to wake up here this morning. The dream felt so very real, real in the sense that when I woke up it took me a while to work out where I was. I almost couldn't distinguish between the dream and here. This is very troubling Kal, that's why I called you. It's like being part of two realities. I feel that I am being pulled in two directions.'

Kal leant forward and put his coffee cup down on to the table in front of him, then he leant back in his armchair, placed both elbows on the arms of the chair, touched the ends of his fingers together to make a triangle and looked at me with a serious countenance. 'They are trying to take you back James.'

This was the first time that Kal has called me by my name since my first day here. 'What do you mean, *take me back*. How can they take me back. I died and came here, didn't I?'

'Tell me about the dream. I think that then you will understand.'

'Well, as I say, it has been going on for a few weeks. I didn't think anything of it at first; I usually forget all about it soon after I wake up. Recently, though, it has become intense and can't be forgotten easily. It has become less like the vagueness or surrealism of a dream and has become more vivid: I'm much more aware of what's happening than in a normal dream. That's why I thought that I should talk to you about it.'

'Go on,' said Kal, 'describe what you see in the dream.'

'To begin with, I didn't know or I couldn't remember. I simply had this feeling that I had had the dream before. Recently though, I can remember: probably because the dream repeats itself in some respects.

'I didn't really want to admit this to myself because I have a feeling that I know what you're going to say. I daresay that you'll confirm my suspicions.'

I took a deep breath before I continued. 'Let's face facts Kal, I keep waking up in a hospital bed. I'm not always facing the same way ... perhaps they are moving me in the bed. I've read about this. Moving the patient helps to avoid the worst of bed sores.

'On occasions, I wake up lying on my back. There are wires and tubes all over the place, several of which are attached to me at various points of my anatomy. Faces peer down at me, asking me questions, sometimes the same questions. They are doctors and nurses, aren't they Kal? What you've just said confirms my suspicions. As I've already said I didn't want to admit it, but the nature, frequency and vividness of the dream tells me what is obvious: at this rate, I am likely to wake up in this hospital bed - wherever it is - and that will be it. I'll be back! Won't I?'

'It looks very much like that way James,' said Kal. 'It happens from time to time. There is nothing that I can do about it. If this is what your body and psyche have determined as the ultimate outcome of your condition, then there is nothing that I can do. I cannot intervene when it comes to your body's processes and functions. As you know from your time here, there are many things that are in the power of the Guardians; this isn't one of them.'

'But I must have died back there, that much is clear to me. I got here didn't I? I have hardly ever questioned how or why. On the contrary, I've learnt or been advised to accept my reality here ... accept it in the sense that I thought that the several months that I have been here are a portent of permanence. Now I find that they aren't!'

Kal helped himself to more coffee while I calmed down. The gentle clinking of bone china cups and saucers punctuated our conversation for a moment. Kal leant back in this chair again, cup in hand.

'There was no mistake when you arrived; we were expecting you. You had been declared dead shortly after being taken to hospital. Otherwise, you would not have arrived here. I can only assume that someone must have observed perhaps the smallest of a motor response in you. This clearly gave them hope that you might make some sort of recovery, even a partial one. Perhaps your medical case and condition was complex and an incorrect diagnosis may have been made? It happens. When it comes to the brain, nothing is straightforward.

'I also assume that your doctors have included deep brain stimulation as part of your treatment. Or perhaps they are trying other procedures in an attempt to aid your recovery?

'It might be the case that you *were* assumed to be brain dead for a short period of time, long enough for you to arrive here. Subsequently, they must have tried brain stimulation in an attempt to amplify or investigate the motor response that changed their minds about your condition.

'I hadn't realised that deep brain stimulation had advanced that far. I wonder if your hospital is undergoing experiments or trials on some patients? Interesting.'

'This might be all very interesting Kal, but where does this leave me? I don't want to go back. I'm having such a wonderful time here; a wonderful, fulfilled and new life. An *afterlife*, I suppose.'

Kal replaced his coffee cup on the table and leant back once more in his chair with a thoughtful expression etched across his fine features. He stared down at his hands clasped in his lap, then he looked sternly at me.

'I am sure that an error was not made in your case. What I am saying is that you were defined to be dead, dead enough for us if you will. However, something must have happened, you must have done something - although you won't have been aware of it - something to give them hope. They are fighting for your recovery, fighting for your life; you must see that.'

'Of course, I understand that now Kal. It's just that I don't want to go back to my former life; I prefer it here. *You* must see that.'

'Of course I do James. This life is meant to be a better life. That's mostly the whole point of it. But, there is no escaping the fact that your doctors are working on your recovery. They see hope in the success in what they are doing. Your mind is being made up on your behalf.

'From what you tell me about your dream, I conclude that you are experiencing a number of sleep-wake cycles. Relative to there, your wake state is there and while you are asleep there, you are here. Relative to here, your sleep state is when you wake up there and your wake state is when you are here. Do you follow my analysis?'

I nod in reply.

'Do you remember any conversations?'

'To begin with, I heard voices. Lately though, I can remember some of the things that are said to me.'

'Do you reply? Can you remember what you say to them?'

'I can't speak. There is something in my mouth. Well, there was to start with; in the dream, there is something in my throat now. I believe that I am answering, I am trying to form the words - I can hear them in my head. They don't seem to hear. I can tell that because they appear to ignore what I thought I had just said and ask me again.'

'This is all to do with assisted breathing. It seems that you may not be able to breath for yourself. Have you tried to speak to them recently, in your dream that is?'

'The last three times I tried very hard to answer their questions. The questions are usually the same: "What is your name?", "Do you know where you are?", that kind of thing. I think that I must have got some sounds out, judging by the response two nights ago. Last night was even better - for them that is. I gave them my name and answered some "yes" or "no" type questions before the dream faded and I woke up here.'

'Brain damage and coma is a complex area,' said Kal. 'Analysis and diagnosis are not as straightforward as you might think. I surmise that when you were taken to hospital, they must have carried out some initial tests and, more or less, thought that you stood little or no chance of showing any signs of consciousness. As far as your body was concerned, your life was over. Therefore, you came to us. During your time with us, steps must have been taken to stimulate what they had initially diagnosed as a severely damaged brain. Very few patients make even a partial recovery from a coma that results from brain damage; the success rate is low. They are obviously trying, in your case, to bring you out of your coma gradually ... and it seems to be working: what you experience as your "dream" suggests that it has. They must believe that whatever they are doing is worthwhile.

'This, in essence, is what your dream means. I am duty-bound to tell you this. You are making a gradual recovery in that you are awake *there* for longer periods. If this pattern continues, you will be awake for even longer periods and your dream state will become your *real* state. In short, you will soon be back where you were before you came here.'

I can hardly bear to look Kal in the eye as I let the enormity of the prospect of returning sink in. It is what I had resigned myself to, but I didn't want to hear it from Kal and I didn't want to believe it. Kal's wisdom as a Guardian means that matters must be allowed to take their course as he described them.

'I don't want to go back Kal; obviously I don't. Who would?

'Won't it depend on my treatment, this brain stimulation malarky? What if it doesn't work? What if I lapse back into a continuous comatose state?

'If I do come out of my coma eventually, I could be brain-damaged and physically or mentally disabled in some way. I don't think that I would want that to happen to me. I used to know several disabled people, but let's be honest: I wouldn't chose this for myself.'

'Your life force is in a very delicate state of flux; only time will tell what will happen eventually. I can't influence the outcome,' says Kal.

'Will *I* be able to influence the outcome Kal?'

'You will see James. You will find your own direction. You will have to make up your own mind.'

'That's a classic case of one of your oblique answers Kal. I'm not sure that it helps.' I smiled at Kal; I didn't want to offend him. 'Sorry Kal ... I know that there is only so much that you can do for me. You have been my guide and mentor for the past few months; I know that you are doing your best.'

'You *will* find out, I promise you. You will find a way I can say no more.' Kal rose from his armchair and extended his right hand. His handshake is as dry and firm as always.

'Kal, if only my past life has been a dream and *this* is reality? Or perhaps that's how it really is. Perhaps this is reality and the other really is a dream. A kind of reverse of ... oh, I don't know; I'm very confused.

'What really upsets me is the thought of saying goodbye to Anne before they take me back for good. I don't think I could bear to say goodbye to her Kal or to the others, Vincent, Primo and Jim. And George might be wondering why he hasn't seen me in his garden. The prospect of being taken away from here makes me very sad, something I have not felt since I came here. I have only felt happiness since I came here.'

'I understand sir, I understand how you feel about Anne. You should spend some time thinking about what has passed between us. Remember what I said: you will find a way, you will find out what to do.

'By the way, in case you are planning on staying awake all night, you might manage it but sleep will overcome you sooner or later, you won't be able to fight it for long. You will soon be able to make a decision that will resolve your situation: you won't be able to put it off for much longer and you mustn't deny yourself from proper sleep, despite what I have told you about the meaning of your dream.

'Call me in the morning. Sleep on it sir, sleep on it. I'll see myself out sir.'

It is with these tantalising and confusing words that Kal left the room and I slumped down in my armchair. I heard the front door close on my tormented thoughts.

Chapter Eleven

The Final Morning

'Where am I,' I said.

'Ah, you are back with us again and talking too. Once more, welcome back,' said a friendly voice that originated from an equally friendly face. I had awoken to familiar surroundings; nevertheless, I heard myself ask where I was this time. My body was bathed in pain and there was a sour taste in my mouth and my throat was sore. As I blinked myself awake in an effort to focus on the face peering down at me, I heard a voice say: 'Raise him up a little please nurse ... thank you.'

My eyes began to focus to reveal a distinguished-looking, grey-haired man in blue medical jacket and trousers sitting on the side of my bed. 'My name is Doctor Kalvinder Singh,' he announced, 'it is very good to have you back, for a bit longer this time perhaps.'

'Where am I?' I repeated in a weak voice, evidently audible to the doctor.

'Everyone asks that to begin with ... it is very understandable. You have been in a coma for just over six months. We thought that we had lost you on more than one occasion in the operating theatre. You have been on a life support system here in our ICU since you were brought into A and E.' Doctor Singh spreads his arms wide to indicate the machinery that surrounds my bed. 'We tried to tell you some of these facts during your previous episodes of wakefulness, but perhaps you don't remember? Your awake episodes have increased in length during the past few weeks. Perhaps you will be able to take in your surroundings and circumstances this time before you fall asleep again?'

'I'll try,' I said. 'ICU: intensive care unit?'

'Yes. As I say, you have been in a coma. Put simply, a coma is where a patient's consciousness is suppressed and there is little or no response to stimuli. You fell into that category and were transferred to our ICU as soon as was practically possible so that we could analyse your condition and decide how or whether we could aid your recovery from your comatose state.'

'Six months! That's a long coma.'

'Quite long,' replied doctor Singh. 'Some can be shorter and some longer. The length varies. By length I mean the time it takes for the patient to experience their first episode of wakefulness. In your case, you have had several such episodes, but this is the first time that we have had a reasonably long conversation. Hitherto, we have spoken to you but you have made very few replies. So, today is a significant milestone.'

I looked around as best I could and saw that my 'life support system' almost surrounded my hospital bed. Dials and light-emitting diodes glowed and grey cabinets whirred and hummed in their karma to keep me alive. My gaze returned to the doctor's engaging face. 'Six months ... thank goodness I've missed Christmas!' I whispered.

Dr. Singh laughed before he continued with his revelations: 'You are in the intensive care unit of the George the Sixth University hospital in Birmingham. You have gradually been coming out of a deep and fairly long coma. We have been assisting your breathing since the outset, but you are breathing for yourself at present. We disconnected your breathing apparatus a few minutes ago in anticipation that you might breathe for yourself again. I will tell you more about your life support equipment later. I don't want to overburden you with too much information for the time being.'

'Birmingham ... but that miles from where I live. What was I doing in Birmingham?'

'You don't remember?'

'No. A coma, you say ... but I've *been* somewhere,' I managed to say weakly.

'Ah ... interesting,' said Doctor Singh, 'I was coming to that. I couldn't ask you when you came in, so your brother gave us permission on your behalf. So, this is my first opportunity to inform you that you have been taking part in one our research programmes.'

'Research into what?' I asked.

'My team is interested in a number of brain conditions, including those that induce a coma in a patient. In short, we are interested in the brain-machine interface, knows as the BMI. We are working with a team of software engineers from the University; they are developing the software and we investigate its effect on coma patients. Would you like to know more?'

'Yes. I am still awake, although rather weak.'

'Please stop me if you feel tired. We don't want to overtire you at this early stage of your recovery. It will be gradual, we hope, but it makes sense to take advantage of your lengthening episodes of wakefulness when we can.

'I'll try to be brief on this occasion. We can discuss it more later.

'We are investigating the impact, if any, of connecting the subconscious of a coma patient to a virtual world, that is a world that is created by software. We have some evidence to suggest that it helps to stimulate areas of the brain and promotes recovery in some coma cases. Of course, we can only assess results if coma patients recover to an extent. Luckily, you are proving a highly valuable case study. I hope that you don't mind taking part: we couldn't ask you but your brother gave us permission to go ahead because he agreed with our assessment that it was worth a try, the stimulation that is. Have you heard of virtual worlds?'

'Yes, but it isn't my area. I too am a software engineer.' What was my brother doing here, I wondered to myself.

'It is early days as yet, but your case adds to our history of positive results. You have been connected to our virtual world from time to time so that we could take some readings before, during and after: brain activity readings, that kind of thing. There is some evidence that music also helps to assist coma patients.

'The software team populate the virtual world mostly with avatars of famous people. There is evidence that this approach is more stimulating than creating standard, anodyne avatars. An avatar, by the way, is a software-generated being who inhabits a virtual world - oh, you probably know that, sorry. The virtual world that we use with patients such as you isn't a standard one that is available for general use, it has been specifically designed for the exclusive use of my medical team. In a nutshell, we use deep brain stimulation and virtual reality software to stimulate the patient's brain. Hence the various wires attached to your head. Not annoying you, I hope?'

'No, I feel ok. Well, not really, I'm sore all over, especially my throat.'

'That'll be part of your breathing management. I'll get a nurse to give you something to sooth it.

'For instance, we include Elvis Presley, Marilyn Monroe, Martin Luther King, President Kennedy ... these kind of people; everyone knows who they are.'

'I saw Elvis and Marilyn Monroe, she was on a motorbike,' my voice no more than a whisper.

'Good,' says Doctor Singh. 'I'm glad you remember.'

Whilst I was taking in the enormity of what Doctor Singh had just said, he continued: 'When you are feeling well enough – and this could take quite some time – I would be very grateful if you would write down everything that you believe that you have experienced since your illness led to your partner calling nine nine

nine. Or you could dictate it: this can be arranged.'

'I already have,' I stated simply. 'Written it down, I mean.'

This assertion doesn't seem to register with Doctor Singh; he merely looks puzzled. 'Doctor, I feel that I have been conscious. Either that, or I have been dreaming or hallucinating more or less constantly. Can coma patients dream or hallucinate or suffer from delusions?' I asked.

'We are also researching that aspect of the condition. We have evidence that some coma patients experience vivid dreams or hallucinations. However, our evidence to date suggests that connection to the virtual world either overrides dreams or enhances them. Again, we only determine this outcome when we gather more evidence from recovering patients. This is where you come in again.

'The evidence that we have gathered to date suggests that, in some cases, the use of our virtual world stimulates and engages the patient's suppressed consciousness. If you like, the virtual world software does the dreaming for you, by placing you in a dream-like state.

'On the other hand, some patients don't remember anything while in a coma. Even when we detect rapid eye movement, which indicates that the patient is likely to be dreaming, such patients don't remember anything at all when they start to recover. In short, there is a variety of responses to what patients experience during a coma.

'This is the longest episode of being awake that you have experienced to date. So, now that you have been conscious for a few minutes, nurses on my team will re-evaluate your life support system. You may find that they make adjustments to the various tubes and so on, but this is unlikely to be of any discomfort. How are you feeling at the moment?'

'Very strange, I can move my head from side to side but I hurt all over, especially my head.'

'I will look into some adjustment of the level of pain killer that you are receiving. It is this drip.' He indicates a drip in my right wrist. I follow the tube upwards but the pain in my head and neck increases. 'I'll send in a nurse presently. In the meanwhile, I suggest that you lie still and relax. I will be back in an hour or so and we will talk some more about your prognosis.'

※

'Have you had a nice sleep?' It was doctor Singh again. I must have fallen asleep and hadn't noticed. 'Any dreams this time?'

'No. I hadn't even realised that I had been asleep. Did I breathe by myself?'

'Yes you did. This is a further encouraging sign that your sleep-wake cycle is gradually progressing and indicates that you could make a reasonable recovery. We need to discuss this in due course.

'I would like to ask you: you said that you thought that you had dreams?'

'I don't know what they were; they were very real though. Can one dream of escaping to a better place?'

'The literature reports that a number of patients have reported as much. The ego is capable of creating a fantasy world, a reaction to the fear of death, a world of pleasant images and experiences in which the individual experiences a sense of peace and joy. These patients often also report that they were aware of an angelic-like presence and that they met friends and relatives who had passed away.'

'Oh, I see. It can happen then. What was my brother doing here? He lives in Edinburgh, like me.'

'He came down to see you as soon as he was informed where you had been taken to hospital. He has been to see you on a number of occasions, sadly when you have been unconscious. Would you like me to arrange him to be contacted?'

'Not for the moment. It is a long way for him to come and for my partner.'

'She wanted to come, but I think that your brother persuaded her not to. You were extremely poorly when you came in.'

'What happened to me doctor?'

'We are not entirely sure. What is clear to us is that you have developed some kind of brain infection. Something like meningitis, if you like. Your brother informed us that you had been to Africa on business. I would hazard a guess that you contracted the infection there and you were taken ill when you arrived at Birmingham airport from Holland. You returned to the UK via Schiphol airport. As I say, you were in a pretty bad way when you arrived here. We pretty much considered that you were dead on arrival, to be perfectly blunt about it. However, luckily for you, one of the intensive care staff noticed a tiny motor response: you moved one of your fingers just a tiny amount. As a result, we intensified our investigations of your brain patterns and waited to see what would happen. Naturally, we contacted your partner - you had enough information in your wallet and on your smartphone - and your brother, and you know some of the rest. We started the brain stimulation at this point.'

'Could I lapse back into a coma?' I asked.

'I will be straight with you ... this is entirely possible; it has been known. At this very early stage in your recovery, it is too soon to say. I am confident that you will make a reasonable recovery to a greater or lesser extent.'

'On the other hand, I could end up with brain damage and be physically or mentally disabled?'

'This is also entirely possible. The recovery rate of coma patients, in particular if the coma is a lengthy one - as in your case - the recovery rate is rather low. Let's not put a figure on it. The numbers aren't reliable; suffice it to say that we are talking of rare situations where the patient makes a recovery that suggests a reasonable quality of life. You are an intelligent man, Mister MacKeever, you know as well as I do that you could be facing a degree of disability even if your recovery continues at the present rate. It is too early to indicate what kind of disability. It could be significant. We can use therapy to re-train physical and mental skills. As I say, it is too early to say. As we speak, though, your mental skills give me cause for optimism.'

'*Am* I brain damaged doctor? I feel that I am thinking straight.'

'We don't know yet. Time and tests will reveal which brain functions, if any, have been damaged. I can't give you a ready answer at the moment. I hope that you understand.

'I think that is enough for you to take in for the time being. There is one thing that has puzzled us though. You did have another visitor. He only came once, a few days ago. He left a parcel; it is tucked in next to your bedside locker. It is large and flat. It could be al picture or something similar. Have you any idea who might have brought it? Did a friend think that you might like something from your house in Edinburgh? It is all rather a mystery. All that any of the staff on duty can remember is that an elegantly-dressed, white-haired, elderly man asked to visit you. He left the parcel where it has been unopened ever since.'

I felt a surge of excitement when the doctor mentioned the bringer of the parcel. 'If there an address or anything written on it doctor?'

Doctor Singh stooped and rummaged around beside my bed and showed me the parcel: *To be delivered to James MacKeever.* I recognised the hand-writing.

'What can it mean?' said Doctor Singh.

'Doctor, if anything happens to me, would you do something for me please? Would you ensure that my brother gets the message to deliver the parcel to the van Gogh Museum, Auvers sur Oise, near Paris, France? Will you promise me? Just in case I don't recover.'

'Of course, but I don't imagine that the situation will arise. In the unlikely event that it does, you have my undertaking that I will talk to your brother about the parcel. Do you know what it is?'

'Yes, I think that I do and it is a very wonderful thing. Please ensure that no-one, apart from my brother Duncan, unwraps it. The address is very important. The museum will know what to do.' I repeat and spell the address while Doctor Singh wrote it on the parcel. 'I've got *so* many questions for you Doctor Singh.'

'I know. Please, rest now. That is enough for one day. We'll talk again tomorrow morning if you are awake when I visit the ICU. You can ask me some more questions then. I will return in the morning.' Doctor Singh lowered me down a little on my pile of pillows and left me to ponder on everything that he has said as I stared at the ceiling in disbelief.

※

I tried to get comfortable so that I could think about what was happening to me. My guess was that my brain might has been damaged: Doctor Singh said as much. That can only mean one thing: I will be disabled in some way as yet to reveal itself. This much, I told myself, I knew.

I also knew that I hadn't experienced some kind of bucolic Arcadian existence, or gone to heaven, or had an afterlife: instead, *I was connected to a virtual world* during a coma. Did I dream it all: Kal, my friend Anne Frank, Vincent van Gogh ... all of them? Was it all a dream stimulated by the mere bits of data of a synthetic, digital world?

Whilst these thoughts tumbled and crashed about in my mind, I suddenly remembered Jim. The probability of Jim's avatar being created in Doctor Singh's virtual world must surely be zero. Jim died hundreds of miles from here ... how would *this* hospital know to create his avatar: what would be the reason? They can't know about Jim!

And the parcel: is it merely a coincidence? Has a friend brought in one of my favourite prints? How would I look at it in my state? The crazy possibility entered my addled brain that Kal had delivered my Vincent van Gogh painting to my bedside in the knowledge that I waned to donate the picture to the van Gogh museum in Auvers Sur Oise. There is, after all, a space waiting for one of Vincent's paintings on the wall of his room at the top of the stairs above the museum shop. When Duncan delivers the parcel, the museum will get an enormous shock: who is going to be able to prove that it is actually by van Gogh? Even if I could explain the provenance of the painting, no-one would believe me. I decide to leave the problem to Duncan and the museum.

I *had* to find out if it has all been a dream or if I have been made to live in a virtual world or if there is some other explanation. I simply had to find out where I have been and I was determined to find out why it has been so real to me. Were there two realities that I have moved between, or was I deluding myself and it is my damaged brain that has been stimulated to believe everything that it has been told by an unreal world of virtual possibilities? I couldn't make up my mind: I didn't know how to; I didn't have enough information apart from the certainty of my perception of the existence of Jim and Kal and the tantalising possibility of the origin of the parcel.

Yesterday, or what I took to be yesterday, Kal implied that I *could* make up my own mind when the time came. The time has come: I decided on a course of action. I will wait until it is quiet by trying to stay awake until night falls and there are fewer staff. Then, despite my weak state, I will start pulling at the electrodes and tubes that I can see and reach in an effort to be free of my life support system. I can move my arms, so I will give myself a fighting chance to get free of everything that binds me to this hospital bed, to this reality.

I closed my eyes. I imagined Primo, striding up the Pike and I saw George tending his garden. Then I saw Anne, stage-lit in the beams of the sinking sun; she was smiling and waving and saying something to me that I could not hear. These images adhered to the tissues of my brain. I *have* made up my mind, with what power of reasoning and strength of will that I have left. I will soon be free ... I must get back. Perhaps being dead in this world will give me life in another one: I opened my eyes and gripped the first wire.